THE
ZEBRA'S STRIPES
and other **African Animal Tales**

for Rodger Stewart

THE
ZEBRA'S STRIPES
and other **African Animal Tales**

retold by DIANNE STEWART
illustrated by Kathy Pienaar

Our thanks to Linda de Villiers, Cecilia Barfield and Beverley Dodd.
Dianne Stewart and Kathy Pienaar

The publishers would like to thank Louis Liebenberg for the use of the animal spoor illustrations.

NOTE: Where the origin of a tale has been omitted, the original source has become lost over the ages.

Published by Struik Publishers (a division of New Holland Publishing (South Africa) (Pty) Ltd)
New Holland Publishing is a member of Johnnic Communications Ltd
Cornelis Struik House, 80 McKenzie Street, Cape Town 8001
86 Edgware Road, London, W2 2EA, United Kingdom
Unit 1, 66 Gibbs Street, Chatswood, NSW 2067, Australia
218 Lake Road, Northcote, Auckland, New Zealand

www.struik.co.za

PUBLISHING MANAGER: Linda de Villiers
EDITOR: Cecilia Barfield
CONCEPT DESIGNER: Petal Palmer
COVER AND BOOK DESIGNER: Beverley Dodd
ILLUSTRATOR: Kathy Pienaar
REPRODUCTION: Hirt & Carter Cape (Pty) Ltd
PRINTING AND BINDING: Sing Cheong Printing Company Limited

ISBN 978 1 86872 951 7

10 9 8 7 6 5 4

www.imagesofafrica.co.za
IMAGES OF AFRICA
PHOTO LIBRARY

Log onto our photographic website **www.imagesofafrica.co.za** for an African experience

Contents

Introduction

Folktales can be described as fictional prose narratives. They are fictional because they originate in the imagination of the storyteller. They are prosaic in form rather than poetic, and they are narratives because they relate a story, often showing conflict and the resultant resolution of it.

Folktales are not confined to one particular culture. A folktale may appear in a slightly different form in another culture that is geographically nearby, or it may appear in a culture that is quite far removed from its original source.

In the introduction to his book on South African folktales, written in Cambridge, Massachusetts in June 1910, James A. Honeÿ comments that he does not pretend to be an authority on South African folklore. That might explain his use of an orang-

outang (also spelt orang-utan) in the folktale 'Monkey the Musician', despite the fact that these are the only apes found outside of Africa. Similarly, it may explain why an alligator is featured in 'Crocodile Tears'.

Alan Dundes, in his foreword to *African Folktales in the New World* by William Bascom refers to the spread of Indo-European folktales from India to Ireland, or the diffusion of an ancient tale from Asia to native American cultures. Similarly, with many African tales, it is difficult to locate their exact place of origin and they often show the influence of European cultures such as Dutch and French.

In some ways folktales are timeless, because the exact date of the event in a folktale is often unspecified. Yet because of the universal themes common in folktales, contemporary readers are able to identify with them despite the distance in time and space. Often there is not a strong sense of place in a folktale, as it was assumed in the original telling that the audience was familiar with the setting.

Traditionally folktales were performed live for an audience and although the folktale was repeated often, the rendering was never exactly the same on each occasion. In some cultures it was not permitted to tell tales by day for fear that the daily work would be neglected and the storyteller would grow horns. However, if persuaded to perform during the day, the storyteller sometimes wore a hat with horns to prevent this calamity.

Despite the fantastical elements that are sometimes prevalent in folktales, they offer a symbolic means of showing how human beings cope in the world. Noverino Canonici maintains that the simplicity of oral narratives frees the powers of imagination of the hearer or reader and enables the individual to relate to emotions that one would not normally wish to demonstrate.

At times, folktales attempt to provide explanations to questions that young people might ask, for example, why animals look and behave the way that they do, or they offer social commentaries. Therefore folktales not only provide entertainment, but they also fulfil an educational role as they incorporate the history, traditions and customs of people within a particular culture. This was particularly true in West Africa, where folktales suggested accepted means of social behaviour and offered practical advice to the hearers.

Although folktales focus primarily on plot rather than character development, they do highlight the consequences of qualities such as greed, pride and untrustworthiness, which are demonstrated by the animals.

Traditionally, certain animals are associated with particular characteristics. For example, the snake has evil intentions and often betrays its friends, while the *python* is often portrayed as the kind doctor who has a knowledge of medicine. In days of old when they saw a python in the bush, the Nyamwezi of Tanzania would pay homage to it as though addressing a king.

The *hyena* is a glutton and coward in Zulu folktales and because of its simplemindedness it is often an unsuccessful trickster. The *tortoise* is slow, sure and wise and can outwit the trickster. In African folktales the tortoise is rarely defeated.

The *crocodile* can be cruel and sadistic, yet sometimes foolish and easily led into doing silly things. Sometimes it is benevolent, as in a Tumbuka tale where despite being of great assistance to the other animals, the crocodile's act of kindness is returned with ingratitude by the tortoise.

The *springbok* is usually portrayed as kind, taking people to safe places.

Although the *baboon* is fast, it is also stupid and easily deceived by a trickster. The *lion* is strong and revered as the king of the beasts, but at times it is too self-confident for its own good. The *elephant* is portrayed as slow, ponderous, lazy and pretentious at times, and both the elephant and lion can be foils for the trickster.

The *jackal* is sly and greedy and often assumes the role of the trickster. In Zulu folktales, this role is played by the *mongoose* as well.

Trickster figures are found worldwide. Although their prime role is to entertain, they also depict the weaknesses and strengths of human nature, especially the disadvantages of character traits such as vanity, greed and naïvety. Often selfish and cruel, tricksters demonstrate an ability to outwit enemies who have an advantage over them. Sometimes the tricksters are small animals who appear to pose no threat to the larger animals of the animal kingdom and because they move quickly and jump well, they are often not caught.

In west African animal folktales the trickster is often the tortoise or Anansi, the spider, who is the trickster figure of the Ashanti people. Among the Hausa of west Africa, Gizo is the spider trickster. While the jackal plays the role of trickster in Somalian and Hottentot tales, the hare is often the trickster-deceiver amongst the people of South Africa, Zimbabwe, Botswana, Lesotho and Zambia. The hyena plays the role of the trickster (often unsuccessfully) in Sotho and Tsonga tales.

Folktale characters do not have a past or a future and in dealing with their challenges, they realize that the choices they make determine the consequences of their actions. Not all folktales have a happy ending, reflecting the harshness of life and some end abruptly. In some, no explicit moral is spoken at the end of the tale, leaving the hearer or reader to reach their own conclusions.

DIANNE STEWART

The Zebra's Stripes

(SAN, SOUTHERN AFRICA)

According to legend, there was a time when Zebra was white all over without the distinctive markings that he has today.

At that time, Zebra was living in a dry, desert-like land where water was scarce and animals were forced to travel long distances over harsh terrain in order to quench their thirst.

One day, as he approached a drinking hole at the close of day, having endured a journey of many hours in the heat that had greatly increased his thirst, Zebra was barred from drinking water by Baboon who had taken up residence at the water's edge. Unlike other members of his troop who spent their nights on the nearby cliff face, Baboon had built a fire and kept a night-long vigil beside the water, guarding it fiercely.

'This water belongs to me,' said Baboon, inclining his long face towards Zebra. 'You may not drink here,' said Baboon, protecting his territory aggressively.

'How can that be?' asked Zebra surprised, as he tried to bypass Baboon in order to have a drink. 'It's for all of us.'

Baboon was outraged. 'If you want access to this water, Zebra, you will have to fight me for it.'

As he was desperately thirsty, Zebra took up the challenge and he and Baboon fought like cat and dog, with their bodies interlocking.

Eventually, as night embraced the land and brought coolness to the desert, Zebra was able to make use of his secret weapon – his kick – and he thrust Baboon so far into the air that he landed on the lower rocks of the cliff face with a thud.

Meanwhile, as he struggled to restore his balance after getting rid of his enemy, Zebra fell backwards into Baboon's fire. It was extremely hot and his white fur was branded black by the long black sticks of the fire, leaving his body permanently and uniquely marked.

The next day while grazing, Zebra looked at his striped fur and was pleased with it as it distinguished him from the other animals. As for Baboon, he landed so hard on the rock that the fur on his bottom was worn away, and to this day Baboon has a bald patch on his rear end.

Why Zebra has no Horns

(KHOI/SAN, SOUTHERN AFRICA)

Long, long ago, Zebra stood on a rocky outcrop and surveyed the bleak landscape before him that was sun bleached and bone dry except for a few succulent plants that littered the countryside.

In those days, Zebra not only had his distinctive black-and-white markings but horns as well, that were the envy of Gemsbok who did not have horns at that time.

Gemsbok finished savouring the dew from the leaves of a succulent plant and wandered over to where Zebra was standing on a bank of rocks.

'Please give me one of your horns, Zebra,' said Gemsbok. 'I would so like to have one.' Zebra looked at Gemsbok and twitched his tail.

'You have two horns, Zebra. If you gave me one, we could each have one.'

Zebra considered Gemsbok's request but after deliberation he said, 'I have two horns, but I have need of them. I couldn't possibly give you one.'

Dejected, Gemsbok left Zebra and went in search of some desert grass.

As he moved, his lithe, sand-coloured body blended with the desert background until he was no longer visible.

Some time later when a full moon rose in a clear black sky Gemsbok arrived at Zebra's house on the rocky slope and found Zebra sound asleep. Because Zebra was in such deep repose, Gemsbok detached Zebra's horns from his striped head without waking him.

Then attaching the long horns to his own head, Gemsbok ran swiftly away, moving his head from side to side in awareness of his new acquisition.

The next day, when the sun was beginning to slide behind a rocky outcrop in the west, Gemsbok was digging in the rock-hard earth for a buried tuber to eat when he saw Zebra coming towards him. Quickly Gemsbok said, 'I asked you so politely Zebra, if you would share your horns so that we could each have one – in all fairness – but you declined.'

Anger rose in Zebra. He lowered his head and began to agitate with his feet, creating clouds of dust that rose from the rock-hard earth.

'Look, Zebra,' said Gemsbok retreating. 'I now have two horns and you have none. And I will never return them to you.'

Astounded Zebra replied, 'You have a cloven foot and I do not. Because of that fact I do not need horns, Gemsbok.'

Gemsbok lifted his black-and-white head towards Zebra, raising his long, dark horns.

'Only animals with cloven hooves have need of horns,' said Zebra. 'Like goats do. Those of us who do not need horns are more important in the animal world than those who do.'

Family Equidae

→ **The habitat of the zebra varies according to species but they are mostly found in grasslands and woodlands.** The Cape Mountain Zebra, which closely resembles Burchell's Zebra, is found in the rocky terrain of the dry areas of Namibia and the southern Western Cape Province.

→ **The zebra resembles a horse** and it has been created for swift motion.

→ **Each individual zebra's markings are different.** No two are exactly the same.

→ **The intensity and width of its stripes vary according to its subspecies.** The Cape Mountain Zebra has relatively broad stripes but is white on the underside of its body, while Burchell's Zebra has markings all over its body.

→ **A zebra's neck stripes** continue into the mane.

→ **Males and females look alike** but males have triangular canine teeth in the upper jaw, which are used for fighting.

→ **Zebras are herbivorous grazers.** They have teeth that are suitable for cropping and grinding down clumps of grass.

→ **Zebras live in herds** and are sometimes found grazing near blue wildebeest. They do not compete because each favours different grazing.

→ **When a predator approaches a herd,** zebras lift their heads and ears to warn not only their own herd but other grazers as well.

→ **The gestation period is 12 months** and one foal is born. It can stand soon after birth and the foal clings to its mother for protection against predators.

How Leopard got his Spots

One day in times of old, so long ago that it is difficult to remember exactly when, Leopard looked out over the hills from his elevated position in the fork of a tree. All was still except for the sounds of animals grazing and a slight breeze that ruffled the grass and stirred the leaves of the tree that shaded him.

Then Leopard caught sight of Giraffe with his long legs and tall neck but it was his leaf-shaped markings that caught Leopard's attention. As he moved his gaze he saw Zebra with her black-and-white-striped skin, so unique to her that she was not like any other zebra in the herd. He was dismayed that his fur was so dull and plain in comparison. He was tawny and straw coloured, just like Lion and he longed for distinctive markings for himself.

Leaping down from the tree, Leopard sauntered through the grass and was suddenly distracted by a movement ahead of him. Moving stealthily forward, Leopard saw that it was Snake who lay coiled on the warm, ochre-coloured earth.

'I am so sick,' said Snake. 'But no-one takes any interest in me.'

Leopard was surprised by his comment. Then fixing his gaze on the reptile he said, 'It is not surprising, Snake. Because you are so mean, the animals keep away from you.'

Silence terminated their conversation. Some distance away Leopard could see Giraffe stretching his long neck to reach the top of a thorn tree, twisting his tongue around a spiky branch of leaves.

Dejected, Snake began to slither slowly away through the grass, his dark body moving across the earth like a shadow.

Leopard followed him for a while and said, 'Snake, wait. I will take care of you until your health returns.'

Snake stopped still. And then overwhelmed by Leopard's kindness, Snake faced him and offered to do anything for him in return for his unexpected favour.

Leopard glanced again at Zebra who grazed languidly with her herd and noticed her unique markings that resembled night and day, then said, 'There is something that I would like, Snake. I'd like markings on my skin.'

Snake looked surprised.

'My sand-coloured coat is too dull,' said Leopard, disgruntled.

After a while Snake said, 'Listen to my plan, Leopard. I will have to bite you but do not be alarmed. My poison will not kill you. Instead your body will come out in a rash.'

Leopard waited anxiously as Snake slithered closer towards him. The wind grew stronger and whipped the grass around them, leaving Snake's movements unheard. But Leopard did not remove his gaze from Snake as he approached him. Then without cautioning him, Snake bit Leopard. Stunned, Leopard lay down and after a while he noticed that his straw-coloured body was a mass of striking spots.

Then slowly he rose to his feet and shook his body, noticing the distinctive markings on his fur for the first time.

'I no longer resemble Lion,' said Leopard. 'My skin is no longer tawny and dull like his. I have spots.'

And so it was that Leopard and Snake's friendship continued and even to this day they respect one another.

Ingw' idla ngamabala

ZULU PROVERB

The leopard eats by means of its spots.

If one wants to succeed, one must develop characteristics that distinguish one from others.

ZULU PROVERB

Akungwe ingenabala elimnyama

There is no leopard that doesn't have a black spot.

No human being is without blemish.

Leopard Cub

(ETHIOPIA)

It was dusk and Leopard Cub crept out of the dark, dank cave that sheltered the small litter that had been born that rainy season. He was only a few weeks old; too young to be out of hiding and too young to be out hunting on his own.

Leopard cub strayed far from home, distracted by the cackling sound of the fleeing Crested Francolin that led him deeper and deeper into the woodlands. By then the light was fading and as Leopard Cub crept through a thicket he came across Elephant who was stripping bark off a tree. This huge animal with his wrinkled grey hindquarters showed great dexterity with his long, nimble trunk.

Unaware of the cub behind him, Elephant suddenly stepped backwards and crushed young Leopard Cub with his sturdy hind foot.

Night covered the land. A thin crescent moon and a scattering of stars witnessed the life slowly drain from the cub. Then it was silenced forever.

Early the next morning on their return from a hunt, some leopards found the lifeless body almost hidden by the grass and they took it to Leopard.

'Who is responsible for this killing?' asked Leopard, venting his anger.

No response was forthcoming.

Grief stricken he looked down at the lifeless cub and asked, 'How did this cub die? I will avenge his death.'

'Elephant killed this cub,' said one of the leopards, jumping into a tree.

'Elephant?' Leopard looked surprised. There was a large difference in size between Elephant and his young offspring that lay dead on the ground at his feet, with the promise of life snatched away from him already.

Then Leopard said, 'I don't think that Elephant would have killed this cub. My opinion is that the goats were responsible for his death.'

As the sun crept higher in the sky and brought light to the earth below, Leopard left the others and went in search of the goats. As he journeyed though the dappled shade, the shadows provided a natural camouflage for him.

Leopard travelled for some distance until he saw herds of livestock grazing on the slopes of the hills nearby. Stalking his prey, Leopard crept stealthily closer and closer to the goats, keeping close to the ground. Nothing would deter him from avenging the death of his young. The goats scattered when their predator made his presence felt among them on the rocky incline. But motivated by revenge, Leopard took no pity on his prey and the number of goats grazing on the slopes diminished fast. That is how Leopard avenged the death of his cub.

This tale from Ethiopia shows that even today when man is wronged, he often takes out his anger on someone weaker than himself.

Panthera pardus

→ **Leopards are common south of the Sahara** to the southern Western Cape Province.

→ **The preferred habitats for leopards** are thick bush in rocky areas and riverine forests.

→ **The name 'leopard' is from the Latin 'leopardus'** which means a 'spotted lion'.

→ **The spots on this large cat form rosettes** on the body and upper limbs, but are smaller and more scattered on the head and lower limbs. The spots or rosettes are circular in east African leopards but square in southern African leopards.

→ **Leopards swim well,** but are not as partial to water as tigers.

→ **The leopard is one of the strongest climbers** of the cats and can kill prey larger than itself. It has a strong neck, powerful limbs and a longish tail. The average weight of the male is 60 kilograms.

→ **Because the leopard's eyes are close together,** it has binocular vision, which helps it to gauge distances when hunting or climbing.

→ **Leopards often store their prey in trees** to hide it from other carnivores.

→ **Leopards are carnivorous.** Their diet includes wildebeest, impala, reed buck, jackals and storks.

→ **Leopards are solitary and territorial.**

→ **The gestation period is three and a half months** and in Africa, leopards may mate all year round.

→ **On average two to three cubs are born** and the fur of the cubs is longer and thicker than that of the adult, and it is usually grey with less defined spots. When young, the cubs are seldom seen. When the female hunts, the cubs are kept hidden in caves or rocky shelters. When they are a few months old, they join the female leopard on a hunt.

→ **The expected lifespan of a leopard** in the wild is seven to nine years, while in captivity a leopard may live as long as 20 years.

How Lion and Warthog became Enemies
(LAMBA, TOGO)

In the searing heat of the midday African sun, as Warthog led his young back from wallowing in the mud at the waterhole, he came across Lion who was wimpering loudly. Wary of Lion, Warthog was about to retreat and go the other way, but Lion's persistent cry aroused his curiosity.

Cautiously he approached Lion from a distance, ready to defend his young. And then as the sun continued to bake the red earth around him, he noticed that Lion's foot had been caught in a trap. The more he had wrestled to free his tawny body, the more Lion had become ensnared. The struggle had drained the strong beast's energy and as he lay limp and trapped on the dry, brittle grass, Lion flicked his long, brush-ended tail in anguish.

'I have been lying here for days and I have not eaten,' protested Lion. 'Please save me, Warthog.'

Warthog and his young stood still as they looked at suffering Lion.

'My body is growing weaker and weaker and I'll die soon,' pleaded Lion.

Then Warthog had pity on Lion who was weakened by hunger and distress and he freed him from the trap.

As Warthog trotted away in search of berries, with his tail held as upright as a tree, Lion observed his mud-smeared youngsters trailing behind him. The sight of the little warthogs running through the bleached grass greatly aroused his hunger.

'You have so many warthogs in your litter!' said Lion, suddenly regaining strength. 'Please spare me one.'

Warthog replied in disgust, 'I have just saved your life and now you are wanting to eat one of my young!'

When Lion began following them the mother of the litter grew anxious and said to Warthog, 'Lion is a strong, powerful animal. We shall have to do what he wishes.'

As he turned to face Lion, Warthog's sharp tusks became visible as he said, 'When we reach our destination you may have one of my young, but first let's have a closer look at that trap.'

Lion began to demonstrate to Warthog how the trap was constructed.

'How did it trap you?' asked Warthog, curious.

Lion held one end of a long, thick stick and asked Warthog to take hold of the other and hold it down.

'But how was your foot caught?' asked Warthog.

As Lion put his foot in the trap to show how he had been trapped when out hunting alone, Warthog released the stick and Lion was caught once again.

When the warthogs trotted swiftly away, Lion pleaded with them to free him.

'You cannot be trusted, Lion,' said Warthog from a long distance away. 'Free yourself.' 'We set you free and in return you wanted to eat one of my young.'

And so Lion stayed helpless in that trap for days and nights until his once powerful and majestic body grew weak and limp, and death overcame him.

To this day Lion and Warthog are enemies. And if Lion happens to meet Warthog, he will not hesitate to eat him.

Spider Deceives Lion

(HAUSA, NIGERIA)

By the time Spider reached the murky brown river, the sun was already on its westward path. But fishing was favourable and Spider caught a heap of fish that glistened nearby.

Energized by the thought of fish for dinner, Spider scuttled along the bank, finding dry sticks for his fire. Soon the twigs crackled in front of him and he put his first fish on the fire to cook.

Swirls of smoke and the aroma of perch floated across the land and suddenly Spider was confronted by a pair of amber eyes that stared down at him.

'I want that fish,' said Lion, exercising his authority.

Shaking, Spider handed it to him without hesitating and returned to tend the fire, adding more brittle sticks to it.

When the perch had disappeared, Lion demanded another fish from Spider's silvery pile. Agitated, Spider put another little fish onto the fire to cook for Lion. Spider was starving and he hoped that there would be some fish left for him as well. But the more fish Spider cooked, the more Lion ate them.

As the tide came in, the waters of the river began to creep further and further up the bank and Spider became more and more desperate as he saw his fish disappearing.

'He has an insatiable appetite,' reflected Spider as Lion consumed his dinner and tears began to form in Spider's eyes.

'Ha! I see that you are crying, Spider,' said Lion haughtily. 'Why?'

'These are not tears. The smoke is stinging my eyes,' protested Spider.

As Spider cooked his last fish for Lion, Bush-fowl screeched past them. By the time Spider had turned around, Bush-fowl had disappeared and he was dismayed that Bush-fowl had not even greeted him.

'I am sure that Bush-fowl has forgotten that it was I who gave her those feathers with the spots!' said Spider, flustered.

'You gave them to her?' said Lion. 'I would like spots too.'

'It would be an impossible task for me, Lion,' said Spider.

The powerful beast with his flowing mane and strong chest came closer and said, 'But why would it be impossible, Spider, I'll help you.'

Spider could not resist an opportunity to deceive Lion and he quickly devised a plan to outwit the king of the beasts. 'We need an old kazaura tree and a bush-cow.'

'The bush-cow will be easy,' said Lion, disappearing.

As Lion forged a path through the bush area in search of his prey, the wind swept his bushy mane away from his majestic, yet scarred face. Just as the sun was approaching the distant hills in the west Lion returned, pulling the dead weight of a bush-cow.

'Ah!' said Spider. 'Now I need long strands of hide.'

Lion tore the bush-cow's skin with claws that were as destructive as talons and made many long strands of hide for Spider.

'Now we need the kazaura tree,' said Spider. 'But you need to test the strength of the tree, Lion. It needs to be strong.'

'How do I do that?'

'When you see a really sturdy tree, push against it with all your might, Lion. If it shakes, then it is not strong enough. We need a strong tree that will not become uprooted.'

Lion glanced at the trees that cast long dark shadows onto the land, to identify a suitable kazaura. Eventually Lion found a tree that stood as solidly as a rock.

Spider collected twigs and branches for a fire while Lion went to fetch the bush-cow carcass and strands of hide. Spider's fire surged into the night, lighting up the area around him and the sparkling embers resembled the first stars in the coal-black night sky.

On his return, Spider asked Lion to make a stand to place above the fire so that they could roast the meat.

'Lion,' said Spider. 'Our greatest challenge awaits us now. Lie down at the base of this kazaura tree and I will tie you to it. You need to be securely fastened.' With the same dexterity he uses for weaving a web, Spider bound the thongs tightly around Lion.

'Wait, Spider. I still have movement in my hind legs. Make the strands tighter,' said Lion, eager to be part of Spider's plan.

'Are you sure that you still want the spots, Lion?'

'I'm ready for them,' answered Lion.

Spider crept away and made sure that the fire was hot enough. Then he put metal rods deep into it and waited until they were scalding hot. As Spider thrust the first blazing hot rod into Lion's flesh he said, 'This is in exchange for the perch that you stole.'

Poking him again, Spider sneered, 'This is in exchange for my eel that you ate,' and branding Lion again he said, 'This is in exchange for the third fish you stole.'

Lion grimaced in agony as he twisted and turned his imprisoned body that was being burned by the hot rods.

'Now that you have the spots you wanted, I am going home,' said Spider smugly.

The fire died down and darkness covered everything like a blanket. For many days and nights Lion lay immobile until an ant crept over one of the kazaura's roots in search of food.

'Help me!' cried Lion. 'Someone help me!'

'Consider our differences,' said Ant. 'How can I help you?'

'With your powerful jaws you can eat your way through these strands and free me,' pleaded Lion. 'I have not eaten for many days and nights.'

The wise ant said to Lion, 'If I freed you, you'd eat me, especially as you are so hungry. I'm not that foolish.'

'But *I* would never return a favour in that way,' said Lion.

'I don't believe you, Lion. But I will free you anyway.'

In the dusty shade of the kazaura tree, Ant worked patiently loosening the thongs that bound Lion. But he was weak and he stood up with great difficulty.

After a few days of hunting, Lion's strength and boldness returned and he went in search of cunning Spider, roaming grassy plains and climbing hills looking for the elusive creature.

One day while out searching, he met Gazelle who was looking very lean. 'Have you seen Spider?'

'I keep out of his way,' replied Gazelle.

'You're not afraid of such a little creature,' said Lion.

'Look at my thin body. During a quarrel Spider pointed a finger at me, cursed me and I have wasted away.'

'How is that possible?' asked Lion.

'If anyone argues with Spider, he points at him and he immediately starts getting thin.'

'Don't tell Spider I was looking for him,' said Lion, suddenly retreating.

When Lion had disappeared, Spider took off the gazelle skin that had been his disguise and went in search of Lion. When he found him resting on a rock he said, 'Lion, I believe that you wanted to see me.'

'Oh no! I don't need to see you, Spider,' said Lion, disinterested.

'Good,' said Spider. 'Because if you come after me again, you'll be sorry. I have the authority now. Verify this with any of the other animals in the bush that have disobeyed me.'

Lion jumped down from the rock and disappeared into the bush. Perhaps it was true that no animal dared disobey the crafty Spider.

Shumba hairairi chipashupashu

A lion does not feed on grasshoppers.

Wealthy people do not depend on small things.

INTERESTING FACTS ABOUT **LION** ➔➔➔➔➔➔➔➔

Panthera leo

➔ **Lions are found from Senegal east to Somalia,** in east Africa, Angola, northern Namibia and from the Kalahari eastwards to Mozambique and northern KwaZulu-Natal.

➔ **The lion is the largest of the carnivores.** Its weight varies from 150 to 260 kilograms.

➔ **Both male and females have strong shoulders** and retractable claws on each paw.

➔ **At the start of the third year the male develops its mane,** which helps to attract a female during the mating season and enlarges the appearance of its head.

→ **In the bush,** one is able to distinguish between a male or female by the size of the tracks. The male has larger feet than the female.

→ **Lions can run up to 60 kilometres an hour.**

→ **Lions live in prides that vary in size from two to about 40 members.** Usually one male adult lion is dominant and young males leave the pride when they are considered a threat by the adult male. They spend a few years wandering until maturity when they look for a pride to dominate.

→ **The adult lionesses in a pride stay together for life** and are often closely related. They sometimes cross-suckle their young.

→ **Lions are usually inactive for about 18 hours a day,** sleeping or lying around, in comparison with grazers such as wildebeest who graze for approximately the same amount of time.

→ **Lions are carnivorous.** Their diet includes giraffes, zebras, wildebeest, impala and smaller animals such as hares and tortoises.

→ **A lion's life expectancy in the wild** is about nine to ten years, whilst in captivity it can be up to 25 years.

→ **Lions are found in bush and woodland areas,** savanna and grasslands, but not usually in forests and mountainous areas.

→ **Lions mate all-year round** and the gestation period is three and a half months. On average one to four cubs are born, which are blind at birth.

→ **Before giving birth,** the lioness leaves the pride and gives birth in a lair where the cubs are hidden. The young cubs have brown spots that disappear after about three months or persist on the stomach in adulthood.

→ **The cubs stay in the lair** for about a month and a half before joining the pride.

→ **In African folklore the lion is considered powerful and strong,** but often dangerously self-assured.

Wildebeest and Zebra's Friendship

(EAST AFRICA)

It was dawn and the first birds signalled the transition from night to day.

Their calls were carried by a brisk wind that whipped the leaves of the acacias, and skimmed the surfaces of the pools that had formed after the heavy rain.

Zebra and his herd emerged from the shadows and trotted towards the watering hole. Soon Zebra, Wildebeest, a couple of giraffe and a herd of impala drank beneath pink-tinged clouds that dominated the eastern horizon.

Zebra hesitated before lowering his snout into the water. Something he had seen distracted him.

'We need to dispose of Crocodile,' said Zebra. 'He is taking too many of our kind.'

Giraffe seemed not to hear Zebra's urgent plea as she drank the cool muddy water with her long forelegs splayed in front of her. To her side stood another giraffe on guard, his long, patterned neck reaching upwards towards the cloudy sky.

'We are also afraid of Crocodile,' said Impala, leaving the watering hole and moving a short distance away to graze some green shoots.

When Wildebeest and Zebra were the last left at the watering hole, Wildebeest discussed his plan with Zebra.

'If we drink all the water from this large pool until there is little left, Crocodile will emerge and we'll be able to catch him. Then we'll put an end to his devastating activities,' said Wildebeest.

'That's a good idea,' said Zebra, drinking copious quantities of the water in large gulps.

The weak sun travelled its course in a windswept sky while Wildebeest and Zebra began lowering the level of the pool. Eventually when the pool was almost empty, Crocodile became uneasy. He quickly climbed out of the murky shallows and headed for a nearby river.

Wildebeest and Zebra trailed him. When they caught up with him, they began to attack him. In those days his skin was soft all over and was vulnerable to their kicks and bites. Soon large lumps of thick skin began to emerge on the dorsal side of his body where he had been attacked, but it was to his advantage as they turned into thick plates as a means of defence.

At last, Crocodile managed to forge a muddy path into the river and he escaped, relieved to be out of the clutches of Zebra and Wildebeest with their kicking hooves and bites.

From that day on, so long ago, a kinship was formed between Wildebeest and Zebra who are often found grazing in the same vicinity, not far from one another. But they are still wary of Crocodile when they drink at a pool because he is always looking for revenge.

Connochaetes taurinus

→ **The blue wildebeest is found** from southern Tanzania to northeastern South Africa, Botswana, western Zambia and southeastern Angola.

→ **The wildebeest has a short neck** and both female and male have horns.

→ **The wildebeest's forequarters**, which resemble those of an ox, equip it for its migrations. It has antelope-like hindquarters and a horse-like tail and mane.

→ **Each year over a million wildebeest** (mainly white bearded wildebeest) and hundreds of thousands of herbivores such as zebra and antelope migrate in a circular pattern that covers approximately 800–1 600 km. in search of water and grazing. They move to the southeastern Serengeti at the start of the rainy season usually in about December. They bear their young in January and February and then scatter over the southern and central areas. About the end of May when the rains cease, they march to the dry season grazing in the Serengeti's woodlands and Kenya's Masai Mara reserve. They arrive there in July where they live until about October when they head back to the southeastern Serengeti.

→ **Some of their predators** join the wildebeest migration.

→ **Black wildebeest are darker in colour** and smaller in size than blue wildebeest. Although they are both grazers, black wildebeest graze kneeling from time to time.

→ **Usually blue wildebeest are found north of the Vaal River** in southern Africa while black wildebeest are found south of it.

→ **Wildebeest and zebras often graze together.** The superior vision of zebras enables them to issue a warning signal to the wildebeest.

→ **Wildebeest live in herds and they prefer short grass grazing.**

→ **The gestation period is eight and a half months** and one offspring is born. The calf is able to stand, soon after birth and is able to join the herd after a few days. There are more births in the rainy season.

Baboon's Revenge on Leopard

(ZULU, SOUTH AFRICA)

It is a well-known fact that Leopard and Baboon are not the best of friends.
When Leopard is out hunting, Baboon seeks the protection of his troop as he does
not like to be alone in the company of treacherous Leopard.

One morning, in days of old, when baboons inhabited the forests and lived and
slept in trees, Baboon was particularly angry with Leopard as he had been robbing
the baboons of their young.

Feigning friendship with Leopard, Baboon approached the spotted predator as he
lay in the shady fork of a large, spreading forest tree, the long branches of which
touched other branches of spreading trees to form a leafy canopy in that area.

'We'd like to groom you, Leopard,' said Baboon, summoning the other members
of the troop who were waiting nearby.

'I'm not sure about that,' said Leopard. But eventually, although he was
suspicious, he agreed to Baboon's request.

'Climb down from the tree,' suggested Baboon. 'And we can get to work.'

Seeing the great number of Baboons that awaited him on the ground, Leopard was
more than a little uneasy but he lay down in the speckled shade of the tree.

Using his mouth and nimble fingers, Baboon began removing insects, dirt and
general grime from Leopard's skin. To reassure him, he handled Leopard's body very
gently and before long, won Leopard's confidence. In time, Leopard relaxed and

enjoyed Baboon's attentions as he could see that Baboon was gentle and not aggressive, and all fear eventually drained away from Leopard's body.

As Baboon groomed Leopard, the troop formed a close circle around him, obscuring his vision. They dug a long trench in the soft, moist soil, the length of Leopard's tail, and quietly they buried it in the hole, smothering it with soil.

Leopard was so enjoying the grooming that he was not aware of the baboons' activities. He could not even feel what was happening to his tail as Baboon gently massaged his body.

Baboon then instructed one of the troop to fetch enough sticks for the whole group that was gathered around Leopard. On his return, the baboons struck Leopard with their sticks, beating him for all the misfortune and suffering that he had inflicted on them by taking their young. Leopard squirmed on the ground in pain as the baboons continued to beat him and then they left him. Slowly his life blood drained from him and he died.

The baboons had surely won their revenge.

SHONA PROVERB

Zvine manenji kuti gudo ripunzike mumuti

It is surprising that a baboon would fall out of a tree.

Even experts in their field can fail.

Why there is a Kink in Baboon's Tail

(KHOI, SOUTHERN AFRICA)

Baboon, who lived in a mountainous region near the southernmost tip of Africa, once lent Black-backed Jackal some money.

Whenever Baboon came near Jackal's den, which was hidden in a rocky crevice on a gouged-out, ochre-coloured mountain face, Jackal felt guilty and he ran away to hide nearby or he gave the impression that he was not at home.

But one morning when the summer sun rose strongly in a still and cloudless sky, Baboon clambered quietly over the rocks in the direction of Jackal's house and caught him unawares.

'I see you're home, Jackal,' said Baboon eagerly.

Jackal immediately grabbed a knife and he began to sharpen it with great enthusiasm on a well-worn, grey grinding stone nearby. The knife glinted in the bright shaft of light let in by the narrow opening to Jackal's den and when he saw it, Baboon was afraid.

Jackal continued sharpening his knife and when he considered that it was sharp enough, he slunk over to Baboon with his ears pointed sharply upwards and a determined look in his eyes. 'Excuse me,' he said. 'I do not know you.'

Baboon took fright and retreated quickly down the mountain face. Discouraged, he went to visit Bushcat to explain his dilemma. 'Black-backed Jackal owes me a large amount of money, but when I approached him, he pretended not to know me.'

'Don't worry, Baboon,' said Bushcat. 'I'll go with you and together we can retrieve your money. Jackal will not kill you. He just wants to make you afraid.'

Together, they climbed the rocky outcrop that led to Jackal's den, smarting as their feet touched the hot rocks that were scorched by the sun. But as the couple reached Jackal's yard and Baboon heard the sound of the knife flicking on and off the grinding stone, he took fright and ran away.

'Don't be such a fool, Baboon,' said Bushcat. 'A fool and his money are quickly parted.'

Baboon looked dejected. His two trips to Jackal's home had convinced him not to return. 'Come on, Baboon,' said Bushcat. 'We have to return to the den. I am going to fasten your tail to mine, so you won't be able to just run away.'

Carefully, Bushcat tied his tail to Baboon's slinky tail, halfway along. Then together they clambered back over the rocks just as the sun had begun its final journey towards its destination in the west. Although Baboon tagged slightly behind Bushcat, being attached to the cat gave him the courage that he lacked.

As they approached Jackal's house, Baboon heard the sound of the knife grating against the hard stony surface of the rock and he was terrified. In fact, he would have retreated if it were not for the fact that Bushcat had dug his claws into a tree nearby and was clinging fast to it.

Then Jackal yelped so loudly that Baboon again took fright and his body trembled. He then retreated so forcefully that he took Bushcat and the tree with him.

'Stop being such a coward, Baboon,' said Bushcat. 'You'll never be able to retrieve your money in this way.'

Baboon refused to budge from his position halfway down the mountain.

'We are going back to Jackal's yard,' insisted Bushcat.

'No, we are not,' replied Baboon.

Baboon had so lost his courage that he was even prepared to forgo the repayment of the money that Jackal owed him.

Bushcat discerned how frightened Baboon was and so he began to untie his tail that had tightly bound him to his friend.

'I see that you have a kink in your tail now, Baboon,' said Bushcat observing the way in which Baboon's tail formed a loop.

Some say that that is the reason why to this day, Baboon has a kink in his long slinky tail.

Papio ursinus

→ **Chacma baboons are found** from central Angola to the Cape of Good Hope, northeast
   to Zambezi in Mozambique and north to eastern Zambia.

→ **Chacma baboons are primates** and it is thought that they have some powers
   of reasoning.

→ **The Chacma baboon is large and slim.** Its coat is dark brown to light grey
   and there is a short, blackish mane on the neck and shoulders of the male.

→ **Baboons live in troops,** which are led by adult males. They vary in size from
   ten to 200. Because the troop offers its members protection from predators,
   a single baboon would struggle to exist on its own in the wild.

→ **Baboons reside in trees at night** on the plains, but in the mountainous regions
   they sleep at night on rocky ledges.

→ **There is a strict code of conduct within the troop** and young baboons have to
   abide by the rules. They also have to acquire knowledge of the gestures and sounds
   that baboons use in order to communicate with each other.

→ **The gestation period is six months** and a single youngster is born.

→ **Grooming fosters friendships** within the troop and it keeps the animals' fur clean.

→ **Baboons are omnivorous.** Their diet includes berries, fruit, roots and bulbs, but they
   also eat small mammals, birds and insects.

→ **The leopard is one of the main predators** of the baboon.

→ **Baboons can be dangerous to man.**

→ **The expected lifespan for a baboon
   can be 25 years.**

How Giraffe acquired his Long Neck

(EAST AFRICA)

The story is told in east Africa, in one of the countries that lies near the warm waters of the Indian Ocean, that long, long ago, Giraffe did not have the long, elegant neck that he has now. In those days his neck was short and squat, resembling Rhinoceros's powerful neck.

It was a time of drought and famine. The waterholes had dried up, the land had been scorched by the sun and the grazing was threadbare. The grass that remained was dry, brittle and tasteless.

One day, when he was out looking for grazing, Giraffe met Rhino and said, 'The grass everywhere has turned bitter. I long for the sweet pastures that grow after the rains.'

'You are right, Giraffe,' conceded White Rhino, plucking a tough clump of grass from the ground in front of him with his strong muscular lips. 'But it has been too long since we have seen rain.'

'Too long,' agreed Giraffe.

'There are too many animals grazing this land and there is nothing left,' observed Rhino. 'It would be so good to be able to eat the fresh young leaves that grow on the top of that tree over there,' added Rhino.

'We are far too short to reach them,' observed Giraffe.

'Yes,' said Rhino. 'But I have a plan. Let us find Man and see if he can help us.'

So Giraffe and Rhino travelled through the savanna lands, grazing by day and resting by night until they encountered Man. Resting in the dappled shade of an acacia tree they told him their problems and waited impatiently as he considered their dilemma.

'I think I can be of assistance to you,' said Man. 'Come back here tomorrow at noon and I will give you some herbs.'

Giraffe and Rhino went their separate ways. Rhino travelled far in search of grazing, while Giraffe remained nearby.

The next morning, the sun rose in a dry sky and when it was directly overhead, Giraffe presented himself to Man. Looking at Giraffe's coat, which resembled blotchy patterns of dark brown leaves, Man said to him, 'Where is Rhino?'

But Rhino did not return at the appointed hour, so Man gave all his herbs to Giraffe telling him that the herbs would enable his neck and legs to grow so long that he would be able to reach the tallest trees.

Giraffe ate the herbs and watched in awe as his neck and legs began to grow longer. He was amazed by the fact that his limbs just continued to grow longer and longer just like the growth of his neck. As his neck stretched, he moved further and further away from the dusty, hard earth and he was so delighted when he was able to twist his long tongue around the tender shoots that grew at the top of an acacia tree nearby.

From that moment, Giraffe became a browser, preferring to eat the young branches and leaves of trees and shrubs, rather than graze the grass on the ground. It was his long neck that now enabled him to do that.

Rhino arrived late, long after midday.

'Where are my herbs?' asked Rhino indignantly.

'You are too late,' said Man. 'I have given them all to Giraffe. See how his neck and legs have grown, Rhino.'

Giraffe continued browsing, relishing the sweet leaves of the thorn tree.

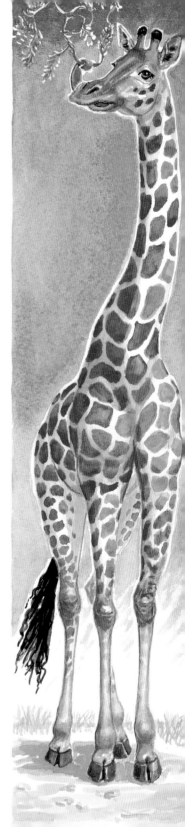

Rhino kicked up the dust with his thick, heavy legs and demonstrated his anger. He was so angry because he thought that Man had deceived him. In fact, he lost his temper completely. To this day, Rhino has a very bad temper and when he sees Man in the bush, he charges him.

INTERESTING FACTS ABOUT GIRAFFE ➔➔➔➔➔➔➔➔

Giraffa camelopardalis

➔ **Giraffes are found south of the Sahara** to northern Namibia, northern Botswana and Mpumalanga Province.

➔ **The giraffe is the tallest mammal in the world.**

➔ **Both male and female have horns,** but the horns are longer in the male.

➔ **The average height for the male is five metres,** while the average height for the female is about four and a half metres.

➔ **The giraffe is a browser** and generally eats above the level of other browsers.

➔ **Giraffes drink every few days** when there is water but they can survive without water for some time.

➔ **The giraffe has a horny skin on the roof of its mouth,** which enables it to eat thorns.

➔ **Male giraffes do fight,** an activity known as 'sparring', whereby they strike each other using their horns as weapons.

➔ **Giraffes are not found in very large herds.** The females and their young form groups and males or bulls, come and go as they please. Males leave their mothers in their third year to join bachelor herds.

➔ **They breed year round.** The gestation period is about 14 to 15 months and one young is born.

Peace among the Animals

(BASOTHO, LESOTHO)

The sun rose in a clear sky and shed its morning light on the peaks of the mountains highlighting their rocky ridges. As the sun rose higher, it's brightness crept lower until it illumined fields of wheat that flourished at the base of the hills that form the mountainous kingdom of Lesotho.

It was the end of the harvest season and Hen, one of the first awake that morning, surveyed the scene from her position on top of one of the wheat sheaves.

Suddenly she heard a yapping sound in the distance near the foothill that captured her attention and interest. When she saw the sunlight dance on the black-and-white back of the figure that lumbered towards her, Hen recognized him as Black-backed Jackal and she was immediately on her guard.

As Jackal approached her throne of wheat, he threw her a greeting, 'Good morning, Hen.'

'The same to you, Jackal,' she replied.

As they exchanged greetings, Jackal examined the young Hen and his mouth salivated at the thought of her succulent young body. He had been out scavenging and it had been a lean night.

But Hen was out of his grasp in her elevated position and cunning, sly Jackal began to devise a way of getting her back onto the ground where the playing fields were level.

Looking up at her with his short, sharp tan snout and pointy ears like those of a fox, Jackal said persuasively, 'Hen, do you know that peace has been declared in the animal kingdom. Imagine that!'

'There is peace among the animals?' said Hen surprised. Keeping her eyes fixed on both Jackal below and on the surrounding areas, she questioned his statement.

'You say that no animal may kill another animal?'

'Yes,' said Jackal, suddenly sidetracked by the sight of a rat that scuttled under a nearby sheaf.

'The chiefs met and made this declaration.'

'I see,' said Hen. But she knew of Jackal's cunning ways and so she doubted him and his word.

Strutting up and down the pile of wheat, Hen repeated to herself, 'Peace has been declared in the animal kingdom,' as if repetition of the words would convince her of the fact.

Growing impatient and increasingly more famished, Jackal said to Hen, 'Why don't you come down from the top and we can discuss the matter of peace further. I am straining my neck.'

Hen looked down at Jackal with disbelieving eyes.

'Perhaps we can even enjoy a little snuff together,' he suggested, trying to entice Hen down.

But Hen was full of doubt and was very suspicious of Jackal's conniving ways. She strutted anxiously on top of the wheat, pondering what Jackal had told her. Every now and then she scanned the horizon, watching for impending danger.

'Hen, you seem distracted,' observed Jackal. 'What is of such interest to you up there? Why don't you come down?'

'Why should you be worried, Jackal? There is a peace pact now among all the animals so no lives are in danger anymore.'

'That is true,' said Jackal, feigning interest in a passing beetle.

'Well, I'm sure it isn't of any interest to you to know that I see a group of dogs approaching,' said Hen nonchalantly.

'Dogs?'

Jackal was almost immobilized by fear. But then the thought of dogs chasing him, caused him to start moving in the opposite direction.

'I must take my leave of you, Hen,' he said.

'But why are you departing?' asked Hen surprised. 'What about the peace pact among all the animals?'

As Hen cackled to herself, Jackal replied in haste, 'Oh! I think the dogs must have missed the meeting.'

Sly Jackal's plan had backfired on him. When Hen next looked, Black-backed Jackal was far down the dusty track. For once she had not been deceived by cunning Jackal. She had ensnared him with her own tall story.

Jackal, the Trickster

(KHOI, NAMIBIA)

Lion had seen many new moons rise since he was last with the pride. After months of wandering and living alone, Lion grew ill. The condition of his coat deteriorated, he lost his strength and he became seriously ill.

He then sent out a message to all the animals of the kingdom to visit him, stating that he looked forward to their respect, sympathy and their gifts.

Hyena obediently trotted off to see lion and on the way he met Jackal who was resting in the shade.

'Are you not going to see Lion?' asked Hyena. 'He is seriously ill.'

'I'm not sure,' replied Jackal. 'If you examine all the animal tracks that lead to Lion's den, you see very few that come away from it.'

'Is that so?' said Hyena, suddenly cautious.

'It's a bad omen,' said Jackal.

But Hyena was not deterred by Jackal's observation and he travelled on to pay his respects to the very ill king.

When he arrived at the den, Hyena commiserated with Lion about his health and then said, 'Lion, I tried to encourage Jackal to come and see you, but he did not want to.'

'He did not want to?' Lion looked shocked and his surprise quickly turned to anger. He was so angry with Jackal that when he eventually relented and came to visit him, Lion used all his energy to reproach him.

'I am so ill and you did not even want to come and offer your respects or comfort,' roared Lion.

But sly Jackal who was known for his wit said, 'But Lion, I went to consult a doctor about your condition.'

At once Lion perked up. 'What did he suggest would be the cure for me?' asked Lion impatiently.

'A hyena's heart,' said Jackal, showing no remorse.

Immediately, Lion struck Hyena's heart with his sharp claws. He tore the skin on his chest and removed Hyena's heart.

The Khoi (also known as 'Hottentot') people tell this story so that those who hear it might realize that it is unwise to get on the wrong side of a sly, scheming person.

The origin of the name 'Hottentot' is uncertain, but it is the name originally given to these people by the Dutch. It is a generic name to describe these people who reside mostly in Namibia and South Africa, south of the Zambesi river. Like the San, the Khoi or Nama have traditionally been a hunter-gatherer nation.

ZULU PROVERB

Impungushe kayivalelwa nezimvu

A jackal and a sheep are not kept in the same pen.

It is not wise to place people or animals together who should not be together.

INTERESTING FACTS ABOUT **BLACK-BACKED JACKAL** ➔ ➔ ➔

Canis mesomelas

➔ **Black-backed jackals are found throughout southern Africa**, northern Ethiopia to the Horn of Africa, then south through central Tanzania, southwestern Angola and Zimbabwe.

➔ **They are related to foxes and wolves.**

➔ **Mainly carnivorous,** black-backed Jackals are hunters and scavengers. Their food includes hares, birds, reptiles, carrion, lambs and fruit. Because they eat carrion, they often help to prevent disease from spreading.

→ **Their preferred habitats are dry, arid regions** and they can survive in places where water is scarce.

→ **The black-backed jackal can be identified by its calls**, which include yapping, yelling and howling.

→ **Black-backed jackals pair for life** and both male and female not only guard their territory but they are both involved in raising their young pups.

→ **The gestation period is two months** and, on average, four pups are born. They are blind and helpless when born. The mother suckles the young but they are also fed regurgitated food by the parent. When they are about four months old, they eat small animals that are offered to them and they also begin to hunt.

→ **The litter remains in the den,** which is usually in a rocky crevice or in an old termite hill, for about two years until the young are mature adults.

→ **The greedy, cunning and sly jackal is often the trickster in African folktales.** A feature of the trickster is that although it is insignificant in itself, it uses its cunning nature to outwit larger, more powerful animals such as the elephant or lion. Sometimes the trickster is of assistance to other animals, but it will always take care of its own needs first. In many situations, the trickster walks away from the situation without receiving the punishment that it rightly deserves, but in some tales, the situation is reversed and the trickster becomes the victim of the circumstances it has engineered. Trickster stories provide entertainment and also have educational value, issuing warnings about the consequences of greediness, vanity and being naïve.

→ **Most traditional cultures have their own tricksters.** Anansi, the spider, is the trickster hero of the Ashanti and related Akan peoples, while Gizo is the spider trickster of the Hausa people of west Africa. The hare often features as the trickster in folktales from South Africa, Zimbabwe, Botswana, Lesotho and Zambia.

Hyena and Jackal: the Cloud Eaters

(SOUTH AFRICA)

Sharp gusts of wind blew clouds across the sky until it was covered by a dense, white cloud bank. Exhausted and famished, shaggy Brown Hyena and tawny Black-backed Jackal slunk towards their homes after a night of scavenging that had not yielded great rewards.

Swirls of dust encircled them and the voluminous clouds that scurried above them seemed within easy reach.

'There's fat,' said Jackal in his mesmerized state. With great agility Jackal sprang onto the cloud bank, leaving his furry, black-tinged tail dangling below the clouds. Greedily, Jackal devoured the cloud as though he were eating a meal of hare or rat.

On the ground, Hyena looked up at Jackal with envy. As the wind ruffled her thick, brown coat with its overlay of sand-coloured fur, she was reminded of her two hungry pups in the aardvark burrow, from which she had wandered quite some distance. She was also starving herself.

'Hyena,' shouted Jackal. 'I want to come down now. Please break my fall.'

Hyena prepared herself to catch Jackal on his descent to the hard, arid scrub land.

'I'll give you some of my food,' he said assuringly.

Eager for some fat, Hyena awaited Jackal's descent. He took some time coming but suddenly he fell from the cloud and Hyena caught him just before he touched the ground.

'Now it is my turn,' said Hyena, so ravenous that her body showed signs of weakness.

Using the strength of her hind limbs, Hyena sprang onto the cloud and she ate as though she were eating the tasty, delicate flesh of a springhare.

'Are you still up there, Hyena?' asked Jackal impatiently after a long time had passed.

'Wait,' she said. 'I am not ready to come down yet.'

When she was satisfied, Hyena called down to Jackal, 'Please break my fall!'

Jackal prepared to catch Hyena as she jumped down from the clouds.

'Are you ready, Jackal?'

Dust swirled around him, caking the windswept bushes and Jackal was not prepared for the speed with which Hyena returned to the earth. Suddenly he shouted, 'Oh! I have a thorn in my foot. Help me!'

And so it was that Hyena landed on the earth with a thud. Jackal had not broken her fall and she had injured her feet.

This tale has been passed on from generation to generation to explain why Hyena's hind feet are smaller and shorter than the front ones.

SHONA PROVERB

Chakakodza bere mapfupa

It is bones that have made hyena fat.

Something of little value to one is of great value to another.

The Great Feast

(SWAHILI, EAST AFRICA)

The feast continued into the hot, steamy night. Shards of moonlight penetrated the thick forest canopy and shone on the animals gathered to participate in the celebrations.

Hyena hid nearby and felt very excluded because he had not been invited to attend the gathering. He recognized topis, Thomson's Gazelles with their beautiful upturned horns and impala mingling with each other enjoying the feast. It seemed to him as though only horned animals had been invited to attend the festivities.

All night long Hyena tried to devise a plan that would gain him entry to the feast that had carried on for days and nights. At daybreak when out scavenging, he came across the shiny tan body of an impala and saw his beautiful curled horns. He immediately knew what he had to do.

With his strong jaws, Spotted Hyena ripped off the impala's horns and hid them in a bush nearby. Then further along the way he found some discarded honeycomb in a hole in a tree and he carried it to the place where he had stored the horns. As he

moved, Hyena carefully held his tail curved over his back and was so excited that he giggled. His plan was succeeding.

Using the beeswax, Hyena managed to attach the impala's horns to his head and as the sun rose in the summer sky, he entered the clearing in the forest to join the revellers. Because they were so involved in the celebrations and they saw Hyena as an animal with horns, they did not see him as being different from the other horned animals.

As the sun rose directly overhead, it penetrated the forest and its intense heat fell on the animals partying below. Suddenly the wax that held Hyena's horns to his head began to melt and he knew that he was in trouble. Holding his curvy horns to his head, he shouted, 'Listen here, everybody! Hold on to your horns! Some of us have horns that are detachable!'

Hyena did not realize the stupidity of his comments. In owning up to his deceitful ways, he had hoped to find an ally but he quickly discovered that there was no-one else in the same predicament as himself. All the animals present in the forest had horns that were permanent.

'Cheat! Get out of here!' cried the horned animals, chasing him out of the clearing.

With his tail fixed firmly between his legs, Hyena slunk away in disgrace, before he had had time to really enjoy the feast.

Hyena, Lion and Leopard Trick Donkey
(ETHIOPIA)

Rain was scarce in the land. It had been many months since dark grey clouds had gathered in the sky and poured life-giving water onto the parched earth below. The animals had little food and their ribs had begun to show through their skin.

'Why is there this drought?' the animals asked one another repeatedly. Hyena, Lion, Leopard and Donkey spent much time debating what had caused it.

'It is because one of us is guilty of sinning,' said one of the animals. 'God would not have caused this to happen to us if we were free of sin.'

'Well, let us confess our wrongdoings and repent of them,' suggested one of them.

All the animals were so desperate about the situation that they agreed to do this. Bold Lion spoke up first.

'I am definitely guilty of a terrible sin,' said Lion. 'It happened somewhere near the village. I saw a handsome young bull and I caught it and ate it.'

All the animals feared Lion because he was so strong, so they listened to his confession and then said, 'But Lion, that is not a sin!'

Leopard slunk forward and was the next to make his confession.

'I know that I have committed a really bad sin. One day, when I was hunting in the valley, I came across a goat that had strayed from the herd. I was so hungry that I drew alongside it, caught it and ate it,' said Leopard.

As the animals were all in awe of Leopard because of his superior hunting skills, they listened to his confession and then said, 'Leopard, that is not a sin!'

Hyena then said, 'I have a terrible confession to make. It was early one morning at dawn when I crept into the village and stole a chicken. I then took it away and ate it.'

'But, Hyena,' said the animals. 'That is really not a sin.'

Donkey was the last of the animals to speak. 'One hot day when my master and I were travelling along the road, he saw a friend and they stopped to talk to each other. They took so long that I moved to the road's edge and ate a few stalks of grass.'

Hyena, Lion and Leopard looked at each other, wondering how they would react to Donkey's confession. In the unspoken silence, they realized that none of them were in awe of Donkey or admired him in any way.

Then they all said, 'Donkey, you have committed a terrible sin. It is because of you that we are having to endure these hardships!' And so it was, that Hyena, Lion and Leopard, showing no compassion, drew close to Donkey and ate him.

INTERESTING FACTS ABOUT **SPOTTED HYENA**

Crocuta crocuta

→ **The spotted hyena is found** from the Sahel to southern Africa, except equatorial west and central Africa. It is not common in South Africa.

→ **The spotted hyena is also known as the laughing hyena** as it 'laughs' with anticipation while engaged in a kill. It is also known to 'giggle' when pursued by lions.

→ **It is strongly built** with shoulders that slope downwards to its hind legs. It has a short, tan-coloured coat with black spots and a short mane.

→ **The female is usually larger and stronger** than the male and tends to weigh more.

→ **Spotted hyenas are found** in savannas, grasslands, woodlands and forest edges.

→ **One or two cubs are born** after a gestation period of four months.

→ **Although the female provides milk for its young** for about a year, the cubs begin to eat meat from about eight months.

→ **Spotted hyenas are often considered garbage collectors** as their strong jaws and teeth enable them to feed on bones, resulting in white, calcium-enriched droppings.

How Porcupine acquired his Quills

There was a time long ago, when Porcupine did not have quills.

Early one morning at dawn, when Porcupine and Jackal were returning home after staying out all night, a strong wind suddenly whipped the landscape into motion. The branches of trees fought hard against the wind that threatened to uproot them and shrubs moved in a circular manner, blown this way and that by the strong wind. A blanket of dust coated the land.

Despite the weather, Porcupine and Jackal continued on their journey home together and vain Porcupine mentioned to Jackal that if all the animals on the earth were as handsome as he was, life would be far more pleasant for everyone.

Porcupine's vanity angered Jackal and as they walked through the windswept grasslands, cunning Jackal devised a scheme to put an end to it.

'Porcupine,' said Jackal, turning to face his friend as they faced the wind together. 'There is someone living in that thorn bush over there who can make you even more good looking than you already are!'

'Really?' said Porcupine, very interested in Jackal's proposition.

'Yes,' said Jackal affirmatively. 'And I'm sure that he would be very willing to help you.'

Eager anticipation rose in Porcupine as he considered the implications of Jackal's suggestion. The thought of becoming even more handsome excited him.

'But Porcupine,' said Jackal. 'I think that you should leave your beautiful coat of fur with me. I'll look after it for you.'

Porcupine did not really want to do that but his thoughts were focused on becoming even more beautiful and this impaired his judgement.

In obedience, Porcupine did what Jackal asked of him and took off his handsome fur coat.

He then trampled through the thick bush that was full of spiky thorns and in no time, his back was covered with the long sharp, black-and-white spikes that he could not remove.

When he made his way back to the scheming Jackal, he said, 'Porcupine, since you cannot put on your beautiful coat of fur over those long black-and-white spikes, I shall have to take ownership of it and wear it myself!'

And so, even today, Jackal has a shiny, handsome fur coat while Porcupine has a coat of long ugly quills.

From that day, Porcupine has never been vain again. He no longer boasts of his good looks as he has lost them.

INTERESTING FACTS ABOUT **PORCUPINE**

Hystrix africaeaustralis

- → **Porcupines are found throughout southern Africa**, southern Kenya, southern Uganda and Tanzania towards the Congo River mouth.
- → **Porcupines are large rodents,** with rounded heads and small eyes.
- → **They have spines and black-and-white quills** that cover their backs, crown and flanks. Dark brown to black hair covers the rest of their bodies.
- → **When in trouble,** the porcupine stamps its feet and lifts its quills while grunting and shaking the quills of its tail. If this strategy is not successful, it charges its enemy, going backwards. Porcupine quills can cause wounds that fester and turn septic.
- → **Porcupines are nocturnal and solitary.** During the day they reside in burrows or in the crevices of rocks.
- → **Their diet includes** berries, roots, bulbs, wild fruit and they are known to chew on old bones to obtain the minerals they need.
- → **The gestation period is about two to three months** and litters of one to three are born during the rainy season.

Why Hippopotamus lives in the Water
(NIGERIA)

Long ago when there were more animals on the African continent than there are now and they lived their lives without the threat of danger or extinction, a hefty Hippo lived in southern Nigeria with his seven healthy wives.

They had taken up residence at a place where rain was a frequent visitor, the river flowed year round and grazing was always in good supply.

From time to time Hippo prepared a feast for those who lived in that area, offering good food and wine from the palms that flourished along the riverbanks. On each occasion when all were assembled and desperate to partake of the glorious food on offer, Hippo called all to attention and said, 'Although many of you have come to this feast, you do not even know my name. Those of you who are unable to greet me by name will have to leave.'

Reluctantly, they all left the feast table without having anything to eat or drink as no-one knew his name, except for his seven wives.

As he was leaving, Tortoise said to the large and revered Hippo, 'If I do discover your name by the time you hold the next feast, what will happen?'

'There's little chance of you finding out my name, Tortoise. But if you do, my whole family, including my seven healthy wives, and I will leave this land in shame and head for some river.'

Tortoise, who was slow but sure in all he did, was determined to find out Hippo's name. So early one morning, when the sun first appeared above the eastern horizon and cast its long shadows across the land as well as the rivers that snaked through it, Tortoise headed towards the water. The red-billed oxpeckers were already scanning the river front for hippos, who, after being out grazing all night, could

provide them with a meal of ticks. Tortoise did not have to wait long before he saw Hippo and his seven wives walking in single file towards the water.

Tortoise found a hiding place near the river and watched as the hippos quenched their thirst and slid beneath the surface of the cool water, creating large ripples that spread towards the banks. Only their eyes and ears were visible above the water. Tortoise listened attentively but no-one mentioned Hippo's name.

When the time came for Hippo and his wives to leave the water, Tortoise noticed that two of his wives were straggling and they were left behind in the muddy shallows. He came out of his hiding place, walked to a place further up the path that they always took and dug a hole in the grass.

Tortoise then buried himself in the hole, leaving only the tip of his rock-hard shell protruding above the path. He waited patiently and after a while he could hear the lumbering sound of the hippo wives approaching.

As the first one increased her speed so that she could catch up with the other wives, she struck her foot against a hard object and screamed, 'Isantim! Isantim! I have hurt my foot. Come quickly!'

Tortoise was delighted as he had at last outwitted Hippo and had discovered his name. He crawled home and couldn't wait for the next feast.

When the time of the next feast arrived, Tortoise was one of the first to arrive. The knowledge that he had made him feel powerful. Standing in front of the plentiful supply of food and palm wine, Hippo made the same speech that he usually did on such occasions.

'Although many of you have come to this feast, you do not even know my name. Those of you who are unable to greet me by name will have to leave.'

Gathering courage, Tortoise said, 'If I reveal your name, do you promise not to destroy me?'

'I do agree to that,' said Hippo.

'Your name is Isantim,' declared Tortoise. Those assembled at the feast gasped, wondering how Tortoise could ever have discovered Hippo's name. Nevertheless, they were so pleased that for once they would be able to enjoy the feast.

Hippo remained true to his word. After the celebrations, when all had gone home, Isantim and his seven healthy wives made their way down to the river and there they remained. To this day Hippopotamus has always lived in the water during the day, returning to the land at night to graze.

Hippopotamus and Elephant test their Strength
(EAST/CENTRAL AFRICA)

In days of old when animals roamed more freely across the African continent than they do now, Elephant, Hippopotamus and Hare chose to live on an island.

Elephant was an old bull who lived alone in the woodland area on the west side of the island, where grass, bushes and trees were plentiful. Hippopotamus preferred to live on the east side of the island in the wetlands where he could spend most of his time in the water to ward off the heat of the African sun.

Hare chose to live somewhere in between but because it was a small island, he was constantly meeting both Elephant and Hippo on his travels. Hare did not think kindly of either of them as they constantly asked him to do favours and because they were much larger than he was, he had to agree to their requests.

One overcast day, when Hare was out grazing, he thought of a way to get even with Elephant and Hippopotamus. He journeyed to the western part of the island where there were many trees. The lush growth there had encouraged creepers to climb and wind themselves tightly around the sturdy trunks and limbs of trees.

Hare began to pull off some of these creepers, unravelling them to make a long piece of twine. Then he wove together many strands so that the twine was very strong and he carried it away with him.

On his way home, Hare encountered Elephant and cheekily challenged him in this way, 'Elephant, who do you think has more strength? You or I?'

Elephant looked scornfully at Hare. 'What a question,' he said. 'If I chose to stamp on you, you would be dead in a second.'

'I don't think so, Elephant. Let us have a contest to test our strength,' said Hare, undoing his creeper twine.

Offering Elephant one end, he asked Elephant to tie it around his leg.

'We'll have a tug of war,' said Hare. 'I will go to the trees in the centre of the island and when I pull on the creeper twine three times, you will start pulling with all your might.'

Elephant was reluctant, but he wound the creeper around his wrinkled grey leg while Hare sprinted away.

Unbeknown to him, Hare ran to the other side of the island where he found Hippopotamus, submerged in the muddy water.

'Hippo, who would you say is the stronger of us two?'

'Don't waste my time, stupid Hare. You know the answer already.'

'Let's prove that you are stronger than me,' suggested Hare, watching Hippo stomping along the bottom of the river, unsettling the mud.

Although he was reluctant to take part in Hare's contest, Hippo eventually agreed and as he climbed out of the water his reddish body glistened.

'Here, tie this end of the creeper around your belly, Hippo,' said Hare. 'And when I pull on the creeper twine three times, you can start pulling.'

Hare sprinted back to the place of the trees in the centre of the island and pulled three times on the creeper twine.

On the west side of the island, Elephant pulled with all his might, taking strain. On the east side of the island, Hippo tugged as hard as he could, moving between the water and higher up the bank, depending on how strongly he was being pulled.

From a vantage point amongst the trees, Hare observed the struggle taking place and it brought him great pleasure. When he sensed that he had got the better of both Hippo and Elephant, he suddenly cut the twine in the middle.

Hippo fell backwards into the murky water and bold Elephant fell forward, making him very angry.

And so it was that Hare took his revenge on Hippo and Elephant, but from then on, it was very difficult to avoid Elephant and Hippopotamus on that small island and poor Hare lived in fear.

Hippopotamus amphibius

→ **The hippopotamus is found in sub-Saharan Africa** in lakes, rivers and swamps. It is only common in regions that are protected.

→ **The name 'hippopotamus' derives** from the Greek, which means a 'river horse'.

→ **The hippopotamus is a herbivorous grazer** that feeds mainly at night.

→ **During the day hippopotami socialize in water** in herds that vary in size from about ten to 40.

→ **The hippopotamus spends long hours submerged** under the water as a protection against the sun.

→ **The hippopotamus secretes a fluid trough the pores of its sensitive skin,** which acts as a sunscreen and antibiotic. It is red in the common hippopotamus and a lighter tone in the pygmy hippopotamus.

→ **An adult can consume** as much as 130 kilograms of plant material a night.

→ **Adult males guard** their territory fiercely, marking their dominance with urine and dung.

→ **The adult male's incisors and canines** in the lower jaw, which resemble tusks, are not used for feeding, but for fighting. The hippo uses its strong lips to tear up plant material.

→ **The 'yawn' of a hippopotamus** is an aggressive tactic that signals the animal's desire to fight.

→ **As the hippopotamus walks along the river or pool,** it stirs up the bottom enabling fish and other creatures to obtain food.

→ **Egrets and oxpeckers are often found** on the back of the hippopotamus and they help to deter flies and ticks.

→ **The hippopotamus is a polygynous breeder.** After a gestation period of seven and a half months, one calf is born.

Huberta, South Africa's famous hippopotamus

→ Huberta was born at Lake St. Lucia in Zululand and embarked on a four-year journey, which brought her fame and took her south through KwaZulu-Natal and then finally to the Eastern Cape. Travelling through the sugar cane fields, she arrived at Durban early in 1929, where she resided in swamps and golfcourses. In April 1931 she was killed by three hunters in the Keiskamma River near King William's Town. Her preserved body may be seen in the town at the Kaffrarian Museum.

The Marriage of Elephant and the Rain

(SAN, SOUTHERN AFRICA)

The story of the marriage between Quap, the Elephant, and Xamus, the Rain, is told that at first they were content, but soon they clashed and had disagreements.

Rain maintained that she provided life to all living things, while Elephant insisted that he was the mightiest of all that lived.

To prove his strength, Elephant twisted his long muscular trunk around a large, sturdy mopani tree, uprooting it and trumpeting so loudly that it drowned the thud of the tree as it slumped to the ground.

Rain who wore the rainbow draped around her waist, observed him angrily and wondered whether she should strike him with her lightning tongue. These thoughts continued as she saw the leaves of the mopani tree shrivel and lose their life.

Elephant who was proud, observed Rain from a distance and began to believe that she was fearful of his might and loud trumpeting. He increased the volume, trumpeting even louder and he summoned the animals to witness how Rain shook in his presence.

Before the animals arrived, Rain spoke harshly to Elephant, reproaching him for his boastful nature and warning him that it might one day lead to his death. Then she packed her things and prepared to go away.

Elephant said to Rain, 'I do not need you. The roots and bulbs in this area are enough to provide me with all the moisture I need to survive and I can also visit the swampy areas.'

Rain did not respond, but continued journeying to her own people. She flashed her rainbow belt in an arc over the dry land and left, taking her rainmaking properties with her.

Elephant relished the tranquillity and peace until hunger overcame him and he tore off a strip of bark from a mopani tree. But it was dry and tasteless and he blamed his parched dry throat on the fact that it had become that way because of all the arguments with his wife, Rain.

'I will go to the swamp tonight,' thought Elephant noticing the dry sky. But when he reached the swampy area, he saw only dry fissures and it was as dry as a desert. Then Elephant started digging frantically for bulbs but found them bone dry as well. Parched, Elephant searched everywhere for moisture, and overcome by heat and thirst he took some rest in the shade of a tree.

As he lay dehydrating in the heat, Elephant could feel his skin shrivelling and he moaned loudly in discomfort, until he heard a whistling sound that distracted him.

'It's you, Xan-bib,' he said. 'Please, Bush Korhaan, take these white beads that my wife made and give them to her and tell her that I need to see her at once.'

With great effort Elephant removed the beads from around his neck and gave them to Korhaan. 'Man-with-the-whistle, when my wife sees these beads she will realize that I have sent you as a messenger.'

Bush Korhaan ran through the dry terrain as fast as his legs could carry him and delivered the message to Rain.

'I shall not return to him,' said Rain, thundering so loudly that Korhaan was startled.

Korhaan ran back through the dust as fast he could and reported to Elephant that his wife would not return. 'She will not come back,' said Korhaan.

Almost too weak to move, Elephant told Korhaan how useless he was and he ordered him to leave.

Sensing Elephant's slow demise, Parson-crow hovered around, hoping for a meal of carrion. Elephant who was desperately weak said, 'Please place these white beads around your neck and tell my wife to return. There is no moisture here at all and I am dying of thirst. '

Parson-crow undertook the long journey to Rain, on behalf of Elephant, and while resting on the branch of a tree, she delivered the message to Rain. Rain became so angry that she struck the tree in half with her lightning tongue. This frightened Parson-crow so much that she flew swiftly to another tree nearby and repeated the same message.

Rain was so furious that she used her lightning tongue in the same way again, striking that tree in half as well. But knowing Elephant's plight, Parson-crow flew to another tree and persisted with Elephant's message, repeating it over and over again. Eventually Rain relented and instructed Parson-crow to tell Elephant that she would return.

Elephant waited eagerly for the return of his wife. When Rain arrived, clothed in a dark grey blanket and imparting the arid smell of rain to the dry air, Elephant was extremely weak. He could not raise himself up from the hole in which he lay. But the heavens opened, rain fell and Elephant quenched his thirst. But as he drank copious amounts of water, it all flowed through him.

Those who had gathered round felt compassion for Elephant and made a grass plug to prevent the water from draining out of him. This was at a time when Elephant had no tail. But he couldn't stop drinking and when he was full, the plug burst out.

Then they put in a piece of wood that resembled a log. It did not fall out as it was wedged in tightly and Elephant was able to stand up on shaky legs.

Rain hovered nearby and reproached him. 'Elephant, the boastful one,' she said, 'I have always warned you against being conceited. If I had not returned you would have died.'

Elephant had no words for Rain. 'From this day, that log will be your tail,' said Rain.

Elephant lowered his head and walked away. He was yet to discover that in a little hollow at the foot of a mountain nearby, Rain had left a pool of rainwater for him.

Akukho ndlovu isindwa ngum-boko wayo

There is no elephant that is burdened by its trunk.

Every man should be able to bear his own burdens.

INTERESTING FACTS ABOUT **ELEPHANT** ➔➔➔➔➔➔➔➔

Loxodonta africana

➔ **There are two sub-species** of African elephant:

➔ **The savanna (bush) elephant:** *Loxodonta africana* is found widely in sub-Saharan Africa and reserves in Kenya, Tanzania, Zimbabwe, Botswana, Namibia and South Africa.

➔ **The forest elephant:** *Loxodonta africana cyclotis* is found in small numbers from Mauritania to eastern Zaire.

➔ **The elephant is the largest living, land mammal** in the world.

➔ **The average male elephant** weighs 5 000 kilograms. The average female elephant weighs 3 000 kilograms.

➔ **A bull elephant consumes** between 100 and 200 kilograms of food a day and about 200 litres of water.

➔ **The elephant's intestines** are about 18 metres long and its heart can weigh up to 27 kilograms.

→ **Elephants are herbivorous,** consuming leaves, fruit, bark and grass. They are both grazers and browsers, night and day-time feeders and some bull elephants push over trees. Elephants digest only half of what they eat.

→ **They are found in a variety of habitats** from forest to open grass woodlands.

→ **One calf is born after a gestation period** of 22 months (the longest period for a mammal). At birth, the calf's umbilical cord is severed, but it is still covered by a foetal sac. The mother elephant peels back this membrane with her trunk and within 30 minutes the calf can stand and suckle.

→ **Elephants live in herds** or family groups with at least one adult female and young calves. When they are about ten years' old, male elephants leave the group. Sometimes these groups contain up to 50 members.

→ **The elephant's trunk,** which is boneless, is a fusion of the nose and upper lip and is not only used for smell. It is used when drinking to suck up water and spray it into the elephant's mouth. It is also used for collecting and uprooting grass, for reaching the highest branches when the animal is browsing and it can uproot bushes and trees.

→ **The elephant's eye** is small compared with its large head and its sense of sight is limited.

→ **The elephant has a good sense of hearing** and its large ears, when flapped, help to reduce its body temperature.

→ **Elephants cannot run,** but they walk rapidly, climb and are good swimmers. In deep water, they may swim long distances using their trunks as a periscope above water level.

Why Warthog has Small Tusks

(ZAMBIA)

Amongst the Baila people, a story has been passed on through the oral tradition to explain why Warthog has small tusks.

There was a time, long, long ago, when Elephant's nephew, Warthog, had handsome long, curved tusks and Warthog's uncle, Elephant, had shorter tusks that curved upwards.

Both Elephant and Warthog lived harmoniously together in an area of open grasslands where there were clumps of bushes and trees that provided favourable grazing for both browsers and grazers.

But one day, Warthog and Elephant had a disagreement and mud-caked Warthog said to his uncle, Elephant, 'You offered to find food for me in your foraging trip through the grasslands. But you have broken your word.'

The friendship was strained between these two relatives for some time, but their differences were settled and Warthog and Elephant became friends again. But when out feeding in the grasslands together, Elephant spent more and more time admiring Warthog's long curved tusks and day by day he became more envious of them.

Eventually Elephant lumbered up to Warthog who was on his knees, trying to uproot a tuber and said, 'Let us exchange tusks for a while, Warthog, and then I will return them to you on an appointed day.'

Knowing that it would only be for a short period of time, Warthog agreed to exchange tusks with Elephant and they met late one afternoon in the shady overhang of a large tree as the sun began to disappear behind the western hills. After their exchange of tusks Warthog went on grazing and his life continued.

Elephant, however, was so enjoying his longer tusks that he had no intention of returning them to Warthog. The appointed day arrived for Elephant to return his tusks and he kept well away from his nephew, grazing and browsing far from where Warthog lived.

From sunrise to sunset, Warthog waited for Elephant to arrive. When he realized that he had been let down by his large uncle, Warthog went off to find him.

When he found Elephant uprooting a clutch of grass with his trunk, Warthog demanded that Elephant return his tusks. 'That was the agreement,' said Warthog with a sense of urgency.

'Sorry, Warthog,' said Elephant. 'I like these better and our exchange has become a permanent arrangement.'

Warthog was both disappointed and dismayed. Looking up at Elephant who was walking away in the opposite direction, Warthog said, 'You have deceived me, Elephant. I am going to sleep in a burrow from this day on, but you will wander far and wide, from day to day.'

As Elephant walked away with his new set of tusks, Warthog shouted after him, 'And from this day on, we shall never be friends.'

Warthog felt so inferior and lost without his long, curved, white tusks that he spent much time hiding underground. One day he went to consult Ant-bear who received him warmly, offering him hospitality in his burrow.

And even to this day, Warthog and his kind are frequently found in the burrows of ant-bears.

Phacochoerus aethiopicus

→ **Warthogs may be found throughout the Sahel** and south to the limits of savanna in South Africa.

→ **Warthogs are so named** because of the warts that appear on their faces. The males have more warts than the females.

→ **Both boar and sow warthogs** have protruding tusks that are used for digging out roots and tubers. They are herbivorous and their diet includes berries, bark, roots and grasses.

→ **Their sharp tusks are also used to ward off** predators such as cheetahs, lions, leopards and wild dogs.

→ **Warthogs often sleep in old aardvark or ant-bear burrows.** The young enter head first but the adult, who enters last, enters backwards so that its tusks can be used to ward off an attack.

→ **The eyes of the warthog are set high and quite far back** on its forehead, enabling it to be on the look out for predators. However, its eyesight is poor in comparison with its sense of smell and hearing.

→ **Because of its short neck,** a warthog often kneels in order to feed.

→ **It is thought that warthogs hold their tails up vertically** so that the young in the litter can follow the adults when the grass is tall. Warthogs travel in family groups called 'sounders'.

→ **Although the adult warthog is black or grey,** it may appear to be red or sometimes yellow due to the mud that clings to its body.

→ **A litter of two to four young** is born after a gestation period of five and a half months.

Why Tortoise's Shell is Cracked

(BAILA, ZAMBIA)

When resting on the ground, Vulture regularly visited Tortoise and his wife. Tortoise and Vulture enjoyed each other's company and a close friendship developed between the creature of the sky and the creature of the land.

One day Tortoise was troubled and said to his wife, 'Vulture always visits us here on the ground, but I can never return his visits as I cannot fly. I have never even been to his house.'

'Do not be troubled,' said Tortoise's wife. 'Vulture cannot expect you to visit him in his house because you do not have wings to take you there.'

'But I am troubled by it,' said the implacable Tortoise.

Then his wife suggested that he grow some wings so that he would be able to soar into the air and visit Vulture at his house high above the ground.

'But I cannot grow wings,' complained Tortoise sadly. 'I was born to remain on the land.'

'So, what will you do now, Tortoise?' asked his wife.

Tortoise, who is known to be wise, thought for a while and then said, 'Tie me in a parcel with a little tobacco and when Vulture visits us again, you must ask him to take this parcel of tobacco and use it to buy some grain for us.'

Tortoise's wife agreed and carefully she wrapped her husband in a palm leaf with the tobacco and waited for Vulture's next visit.

It wasn't long before he descended from the grey sky, landed on the ground and arrived at their house. 'Where's Tortoise?' he asked.

'He has gone to visit people who live some distance away,' said Tortoise's wife.

'Alas! We have no grain in the house and he left hungry.'

'That's terrible,' said Vulture. 'You cannot live without grain.'

'Is it not possible to buy grain at the place where you live, Vulture?'

'Yes, there is plenty there,' said Vulture, reassuring Tortoise's wife.

Tortoise's wife then went to fetch the palm leaf parcel and offered it to Vulture saying, 'In this parcel is some tobacco. My husband hoped you would use it to purchase some grain and then bring it home for us.'

Vulture took off into the air, flapping his magnificent wings as he flew towards his house high above the earth. As he was approaching home he heard a voice saying, 'Vulture, this is your friend, Tortoise. Please unwrap me. I want to visit you in your house.'

Vulture was so startled that he let go of his parcel and it fell, down, down, down to the earth with a thud. Tortoise's shell shattered and sadly he died.

So the close friendship between Tortoise and Vulture ended, but to this day you can still see cracks in the shell of Tortoise as a reminder of this unhappy event.

Tortoise deceives Elephant
(TANZANIA)

This story about small Tortoise and large Elephant was originally told by the Nyakyusa who lived in the north-west around Lake Nyasa.

'So, Elephant, you think you are the mightiest of all the animals,' said Tortoise.

'Can't you see that I am?' replied Elephant, detaching a clutch of green leaves from a tree with his agile trunk.

Tortoise thought for a while, and then said, 'I doubt that you have seen your own head, Elephant.'

'So what!' replied Elephant.

'Well, I'm sure I could jump over it,' said Tortoise, seeking a contest.

'You could?' asked Elephant, not inclining his head towards Tortoise, as he was too interested in feeding.

'Yes, I could,' said Tortoise confidently.

'Prove it,' said Elephant with disdain.

'Oh! But I couldn't do it today, Elephant. I have travelled so far and I am exhausted.'

'Excuses!' muttered Elephant as he moved towards the next tree.

'Alright. Let's set a date for the contest,' said Tortoise. 'What about tomorrow?' Elephant agreed and went on stripping bark from the tree.

Tortoise crept away and went in search of his wife. Having told her of his plan, he hid her in a leafy bush at the site of the contest.

The next morning, at first light, as the sun rose in a clear blue sky and cast long finger shadows on the ground, Elephant lumbered towards the clearing, swinging his trunk. On his arrival, he found Tortoise already waiting for him.

Elephant positioned himself in the centre of the clearing, with his head held upright and his wrinkly skin hanging loosely around him. Tortoise stood opposite the place where his wife was hiding in the bushes.

'Hurry, Tortoise, jump!' urged Elephant, growing impatient.

Tortoise prepared himself for his jump and shouted, 'Hi-i!' Then he crept back into the grass. Meanwhile his wife was on the other side of Elephant and shouted, 'Ehe!'

Elephant was confused and looked this way and that. He saw Tortoise on the other side of him, although he had not seen Tortoise jump over his head.

'You'll have to jump again, Tortoise,' said Elephant. 'I missed your jump.'

On the next occasion Tortoise's wife said, 'Hi-i!' and Tortoise shouted, 'Ehe!'

Elephant was even more bewildered. He thought that perhaps the jump had been so fast that he had not seen it.

'I've been beaten by you, Tortoise,' Elephant confessed. 'But let's have a race by foot. I'm sure I'll beat you.'

'Perhaps, Elephant. But not today. My legs are so weak and tired after all the jumping. What about tomorrow?'

'Alright, Tortoise,' said Elephant, flapping his ears to cool down as it was midday and the heat beat down on them.

A place was decided that would mark the start of the race and Elephant and Tortoise agreed to meet at the appointed time the next day.

Meanwhile that night, Tortoise gathered his children around him and he summoned the rest of the clan, hiding them at regular intervals along the course. When they were safely hidden from view, he gave them instructions on what to do.

As the sun crept above the eastern horizon, Elephant walked eagerly towards the start of the race saying, 'Ndi! Ndi! Ndi!' as he set out.

Thinking that he was well ahead of Tortoise, Elephant called out to his small friend expecting a reply from behind him. But he heard a voice ahead of him reply, 'Here I am, Elephant.'

Elephant increased his speed and ran on ahead. Again he called out, 'Tortoise, where are you now?' And a voice replied from way ahead of him, 'Here I am.' Elephant couldn't believe that slow Tortoise was ahead of him. He ran even faster and was so surprised to find Tortoise waiting for him at the finishing line. How was that possible?

Elephant was not sure how he could have been defeated by cunning Tortoise again, yet he had to admit that it was true.

Charova sei chando chakwidza hamba mumuti

The frost must have been very heavy for the tortoise to climb the tree.

It is amazing what people do in a crisis.

INTERESTING FACTS ABOUT
LEOPARD TORTOISE →→→→→

Geochelone pardalis

→ **They are found from southern Sudan** and Ethiopia south to KwaZulu-Natal and west to Namibia and southern Angola.

→ **The pattern on the carapace** (shell) of the young leopard tortoise resembles that of a leopard.

→ **It is herbivorous** and its diet includes grasses, fungi, fallen fruit and those plants that contain a great deal of moisture.

→ **The tortoise retracts its head and legs** into its hard shell for protection.

→ **A tortoise has no teeth**, but its jaws have a sharp edge for cutting and tearing.

→ **Tortoises are the longest-living vertebrates.**

→ **They are found in lightly wooded areas,** open grassy plains, dry woodlands and thorn scrub regions.

→ **The female lays five to 30 white, round eggs** in a hole every three weeks for a period of about five months. The eggs take a year to hatch.

→ **The tortoise is frequently featured in African folklore** and is usually victorious. Its character is portrayed as patient, slow, vindictive and sometimes cruel in revenge. Its slow but sure movements and wrinkled skin give the impression that the tortoise is very old and wise and it is known for its uncanny wisdom.

Why Monkeys Choose to live up Trees

(EWE, DAHOMEY)

From sunrise to sunset, old Bushcat was out hunting, but she had not been successful in finding food, not even a snake.

So, exhausted, she lay down in the shade of an old gnarled tree that was about the same age as she was. They had both known almost 20 summers.

But Bushcat was restless as she tried to find rest in the shade. Fleas attacked her incessantly and she grew more and more irritated. Then, just as she lifted her head to capture the last rays of the setting sun, she caught sight of Monkey in the tree above her.

'Please help me to get rid of these fleas that are attacking me,' Bushcat pleaded with Monkey.

Monkey swung down from the leafy branches of the tree and started picking the fleas off Bushcat's tawny body. Bushcat was so soothed by Monkey's actions that she fell asleep. Monkey then seized the opportunity to tie Bushcat's tail to a low branch of the tree and ran away chattering to himself.

When Bushcat awoke and tried to stretch, she felt that her movements were restricted. Then she noticed that her tail had been fastened to the tree and she twisted her body this way and that, trying to free herself. But she was tied fast.

Darkness was falling and as Bushcat fixed her vision on the ground in front of her, she noticed a tiny creature creeping slowly past her.

'Snail, please untie my tail,' she said.

'You'll eat me, Bushcat,' said Snail, trying to get out of Bushcat's way.

'I promise I won't,' said Bushcat in a reassuring voice.

So Snail slowly untied Bushcat's tail from the lowest branches of the gnarled tree and crept away into the darkness that was just lit by a crescent moon.

When Bushcat arrived home, she immediately issued the following instruction to all the animals. 'Five days from now, tell everyone that I am dead and that you are going to bury me.'

The animals were surprised, but they agreed.

When the fifth day dawned and the early morning silence was broken by the first birds, Bushcat lay down flat against the hard earth and feigned death. The animals danced around her and continued to dance, exactly as they had been instructed to do.

Suddenly, Bushcat jumped up and tried to pounce on Monkey. But Monkey had already sprung into the tree above the animals, thus escaping Bushcat's anger.

And so to this day, Monkey does not consider it safe to stay on the ground, as Bushcat might catch him. That is why he chooses to live up a tree.

Monkey the Musician

(SOUTH AFRICA)

Once there had been plenty of food in the land where Monkey lived. Berries were ready for the picking, insects and scorpions were numerous and Monkey was always well fed. But circumstances changed and Monkey was forced to leave his home territory and live some distance away with his great uncle, Orang-outang.

Monkey found work and after a long time of labouring there, he desired to return to his home territory. As a reward for his labour, his great-uncle gave him a bow and arrow, and a fiddle.

'This fiddle will be very useful to you, Monkey,' said Orang-outang. 'When you play it, you will make anything dance.'

'Thank you,' said Monkey intrigued.

'And with this bow and arrow, you will be able to kill anything you wish,' said his great-uncle.

Monkey had not been journeying long when he encountered Brer Wolf, who had been trying unsuccessfully to kill an antelope all morning.

'I'll kill it for you,' said Monkey, taking out his bow and arrow.

With great alacrity and skill, Monkey took aim and immediately brought the antelope to the ground.

'I'd like that bow and arrow,' said Brer Wolf. 'Please give it to me.'

But Monkey refused to part with the gift that his great-uncle had given him.

Wolf was extremely disappointed and, using his superior strength, he began to threaten Monkey.

'I must have that bow and arrow,' insisted Wolf.

'You are not getting it,' said Monkey firmly.

Jackal came slinking by and Wolf said, 'Monkey has stolen my bow and arrow.' When the disagreement persisted, Jackal said, 'I am not able to pass judgement on this case. But I suggest that we bring this matter to the court of Lion, Tiger and the other animals.'

'Oh! And let me keep the fiddle in the mean time,' suggested Jackal. 'Then it will be safe.'

But Monkey and Wolf did not want to take the matter to court and Jackal had to provide a great amount of food for them before they agreed with him.

Late one afternoon, when the sun was approaching the western horizon, the animals came together and the court assembled. Jackal testified against Monkey and when called to give evidence, Monkey's evidence was not strong enough. Jackal thought that by testifying against Monkey, he would be able to acquire the desired bow and arrow from Wolf.

But Monkey was convicted and he received the death penalty for theft.

'As a final right,' said Monkey in a faint voice, 'please may I play the fiddle for the last time? It is so dear to my heart.'

Permission was granted and Monkey started to play the song called 'Cockcrow'. He was a fine musician who made the fiddle sing and soon all the animals of the court began to dance. And they danced and danced, and the plump, rising full moon

witnessed their joy in dancing. In fact, the animals danced and danced until they fell down exhausted with their feet still moving in the air in time to the music.

Monkey was so engrossed in playing his beloved fiddle, that he did not notice what was happening around him until Wolf said, 'Please stop playing your fiddle now, Monkey.'

Ignoring Wolf, Monkey persisted in the bright light of the moon, playing 'Cockcrow' yet again.

Lion, who was so tired, eventually growled, 'Ape, please stop playing that fiddle. If you do, I will give you my kingdom.'

'I don't want your kingdom,' retorted Monkey, making his fiddle sing even louder. 'But if you rescind my sentence and Wolf admits that he stole my bow and arrow, I will be satisfied.'

'Alright. I admit that I stole your bow and arrow,' conceded Wolf. And with that, Lion rescinded the sentence.

Monkey was so delighted that he took up his fiddle again and gave them another rendering of 'Cockcrow'. And after playing it a few more times, Monkey went and took up residence in a camelthorn tree, hugging his fiddle.

Meanwhile, the animals quickly departed and went to other parts of the land as they dreaded the sound of Monkey's fiddle.

Monkey carries the Drum

(ASHANTI, GHANA)

Among the Ashanti of Ghana, Anansi, the spider, is the trickster hero. Although he is a hero, he is sometimes a buffoon. He is constantly preoccupied with outwitting the creatures of the field and forest, as well as man. Anansi is sometimes seen as greedy, predatory, cunning and without conscience.

Although drums are used to make special announcements, they are often vehicles of literature. On state occasions, poetry is drummed to the chief and the community as a whole.

Some time ago, the king of the forest convened a special meeting and he sent his messengers far and wide to tell all the animals about the important meeting.

On receipt of the message, the animals dressed in their best clothes and set out early the next morning for the forest. Some of the animals, such as Elephant, Leopard and Lion had a long way to travel and they took a long time to reach their destination. Also, it was summer and the days were hot.

When they had all arrived, the king said, 'It has taken you far too long to assemble. What if an enemy arrived in our midst? What if there was a great danger?' 'We need to try and come together more quickly,' said the king in a loud voice.

Anansi, the spider who was the king's adviser, made a suggestion, 'What is needed is a royal drum,' he said, trying to capture everyone's attention. 'When it is beaten, it will be heard everywhere and then everyone will come running in response to the summons.'

'That's a good idea,' said the king. 'A drum will be made.'

He then organized the animals into work parties that would all be involved in the creation of the royal drum.

The first work party went out in search of the right tree for the drum. When they had found it, they felled the tree and watched as it crashed to the ground. The second work party trimmed the tree and finally the third work party was responsible for shaping it into the form of the drum.

There was great excitement as all the animals witnessed the hollowing of the drum and great jubilation when it was given to the carvers to decorate with a delicate and intricate design.

But there was one animal who did not work at all. While the others laboured, Monkey went off in search of berries or he found a shady place in which to sleep. And he giggled to himself as he heard the work party sing, 'We are so tired and hot, but we are working for the king.'

Then Monkey also sang, 'I am so tired and hot, but I am working for the king.'

But it was Anansi, the spider, who noticed that Monkey was shirking his duty. Although he chose to rest while the others laboured from morning to night, Anansi said nothing about Monkey's lack of cooperation.

Once the chiselling and carving had been done and the elaborate design on the king's drum was completed, the king announced that there would be a ceremony to mark the arrival of the drum. Anansi, ever sharp, asked, 'Who will carry the king's drum?'

He knew that the king's prized possession was large and very heavy. He also knew that the distance was great and that no-one would want to carry the drum.

Leopard said, 'I think the honour should be Lion's.'

'I think that Antelope should have the honour,' replied Lion.

But Antelope quickly declared, 'I think that Elephant should have the honour.'

Anansi then said, 'It would seem difficult to decide who should have the honour. Therefore I suggest that the laziest person should carry the drum.'

The king agreed and all the animals looked at one another to try and discover who the laziest animal was. One of them looked at Monkey, then another did, while Monkey in turn looked at someone and then someone else again. But everywhere he looked, Monkey saw someone looking at him.

'Eh!' said Monkey, standing in the middle of the circle of animals so that he could capture their attention, 'I wish to say that I refuse to carry the drum. I will never carry the drum.'

All the animals laughed. 'Why are you here? No-one mentioned your name!'

Porcupine added, 'Monkey, why do you speak? Nobody asked you to carry the king's drum!'

The animals then echoed, 'No-one even said one word to him!'

Then Anansi, the king's advisor, crept over to the king and said, 'No-one even mentioned Monkey's name. They were trying to decide for themselves who the laziest animal was. But Monkey came forward and said that he would never carry the drum. By coming forward, he implicated himself, thus confessing that he was the laziest.'

The king smiled.

'It is true, Monkey is the laziest!' agreed all the animals present.

And so, when the great drum was brought from the forest to the king's house, it was Monkey who carried it.

Inkaw' isina nesikhweb' etsheni

A monkey dances on a stone with a corn cob.

Having stolen a corn cob, it would be wise for the monkey to flee with it. Likewise, it is unwise to celebrate something too soon. One should wait until the danger has passed.

ZULU PROVERB

Ceropithecus aethiops

➔ **Vervet monkeys are widely distributed** throughout Africa, from Senegal to Ethiopia and south to South Africa.

➔ **They occur in woodland environments** and on the edges of forests, in dry and wet savanna regions but not in rain forests.

➔ **The colour of their fur varies from region to region.** It can be grey to yellow, reddish or olive green. Vervet monkeys have black faces with white across their brows and their ears, hands and feet are black.

➔ **They live in troops of about 20 members or more.** There is one dominant male that protects the troop's territory, guides the members' search for food and is on the alert for predators such as leopards or eagles. When the troop forages for food, this male leader, often assisted by other males, remains on guard.

➔ **When they are about four years old,** young males leave the troop at the instigation of the dominant male.

➔ **Like the males, the females have a ranking order.** Young females often remain with the troop where they learn to take care of the young.

➔ **Vervet monkeys can be destructive feeders,** denuding fields of sugar cane and fruit. Their normal diet includes seeds and seed-pods, herbs, insects, fruit and flowers.

➔ **The gestation period is about five and a half months** and one young is born.

➔ **Grooming is an important activity amongst Vervet monkeys.** Not only is their fur kept clean in this way, but it creates a bond between members of the troop.

Why Hare has a Split Lip

(SAN/kHOI, SOUTHERN AFRICA)

As Tortoise crept slowly along the well-worn track, gouged out of the hard earth by the tread of countless animals, the acrid smell of dust pervaded his nostrils. Pausing momentarily, Tortoise caught sight of the faint new moon in the pale early morning sky.

Moon then said to Tortoise, 'Give this message to the earth's inhabitants: As I die and again return, so men will die and again return.'

Tortoise continued on the dusty track while practising the message over and over again. But he was so slow undertaking his journey that by the time he reached his destination, he had forgotten the message.

Turning to the sky and noticing that the full moon was still visible, Tortoise said, 'Moon, I have forgotten the message. You will need to give it to me again.'

Moon was so angry that Tortoise had not been able to deliver the message that he sought Hare.

'Hare, you are known for your speed. Take this message to the inhabitants of the earth:

"As I die and again return, so shall men die and again return."'

Hare sprinted quickly through the dry terrain, hoping to deliver Moon's message before the sun scorched the land with its heat and sent animals in search of shade. But some succulent green shoots waylaid Hare and he also forgot the Moon's message to the people of the earth.

The body of Hare trembled and he was too afraid to return to Moon with the news that like Tortoise, he, too, had forgotten his message. He tried to remember the words of the moon and repeated them over and over again to himself until he believed they were correct. Then he journeyed on towards the inhabitants of the earth.

But his thoughts were jumbled and he delivered these words, 'The moon has a message. Unlike itself, you, the earth's inhabitants, will die and not again return.'

When it came to the notice of the moon that Hare had jumbled the message and delivered it incorrectly, his anger could not be contained. Moon struck Hare on the lip, causing a harelip, which has remained ever since.

Mischievous Hare

(FULANI, NORTHERN NIGERIA)

Long, long ago, Hare was a farmer, like the other animals that lived in those parts.

When the rains came and the lands were moist and pliable, Hare worked diligently, preparing the soil for planting and then covering the corn seed with the rich fertile earth. The rain encouraged the weeds to grow so Hare spent many hours weeding the fields, scaring away the birds and then helping to harvest the crop after months of growth.

The plentiful corn harvest was stored in circular bins, the openings of which were under roofs of grass. It had been a long season and all the animals that had worked solidly from dawn to dusk until their work was done were discussing where they would rest, now that the rainy season was over.

'I'm going to visit my relatives that live in Sittincawbin,' commented Hare. 'It is a long way from here and I shall undertake the journey on my own.'

With the onset of cloudless skies and dry weather, the animals herded together their cattle and set off for their various destinations, hoping to find good grazing for their livestock.

'Well, our grain is stored now,' said Hare. 'When we come back to this place we'll have enough corn for food and planting. Have a safe journey, everyone.'

When all the animals had disappeared over the horizon, Hare crept stealthily back to where the bins were standing in the open sunlight. Removing the dried grass roof of the bin that was first in line, Hare jumped into it, devouring the corn as though it were his last meal. Drowsy, he slept in the bin, waking only to eat the corn and continuing until the supply was depleted.

When Hare found himself in an empty bin, he jumped out and went to collect small stones, which he threw into the first bin to replace the corn. Then he jumped into the second bin and he remained there for many days and nights until he had consumed all the corn in that bin, replacing it with small stones as well.

After some time, when the grey clouds gathered in the sky to mark the return of the rainy season, the animals began to return one by one with their herds of cattle. But Hare was missing. 'That's strange,' said one of the animals.

'He *was* travelling a long, long distance to visit relatives in Sittincawbin,' said another. 'No doubt he'll soon arrive.'

But the days passed and there was no sign of Hare. The other animals became worried and began to search the village, calling out aloud for him. Meanwhile, cunning Hare was hiding and, in a quiet little voice that made him sound far away, he said, 'I'm on my way home.'

Hare returned to his hiding place and waited until the animals called for him again at dusk. He did not need to go out foraging as he had eaten such a large supply of corn. This time he raised his voice so that it didn't sound so far away and said, 'I'm on my way home.'

Eventually, Hare darted to the place where they were all waiting for him and said, 'I am so exhausted. I have travelled a great distance.'

Finally, when all the animals were present, they removed the grass roof from the first bin that had been bleached by the sun and they looked eagerly inside it.

Then they looked into the next bin and the next and the next, and to their dismay, they discovered that their corn had been stolen and small stones had been put into the bins instead.

Angry and dismayed, the animals fought amongst themselves trying to discover who was responsible for this disaster. Eventually, as the day was waning, Jackal said, 'The animal on whom the moon casts its first bright light is responsible for this.' And he urged them all to stop their disagreements and go to sleep.

One by one the tired animals lay down and soon were embraced by sleep. Hare negotiated his sleeping position next to Squirrel and feigned sleep, keeping his eyes open. Anxiously he waited for the moon to appear.

The crescent moon rose in a cloudy sky and its light was not as bright as usual. Hare was the only animal awake and he saw the first shards of light fall on himself. Startled, he moved quickly away, leaving Squirrel bathed in moonlight. Then he began to sing, so that the animals would wake and be aware of the fact that the thief had been discovered.

On waking, all the animals began to attack Squirrel and sly Hare went unpunished.

Wethemb' uboya bentenesha

ZULU PROVERB

It is the fur of the hare that he trusts.

Although the fur of a hare looks good, when one rubs it, the hairs fall out. This is said to warn a person not to put their faith in something that is not long lasting.

Lepus saxatilis

→ **The scrub hare is found in South Africa**, Namibia and central Mozambique.

→ **It is found mostly in woodland and dry areas.**

→ **Because it is nocturnal,** the scrub hare is not often seen during the day. It lies in hollows to escape the heat of the sun. One of the differences between hares and rabbits is that a hare does not burrow. It lies in a 'form', which is a hidden hollow in grass or beneath a bush. Rabbits dig underground burrows.

→ **Hares are usually solitary,** while rabbits are social and live in colonies.

→ **The scrub hare is a vegetarian,** preferring the shorter grass.

→ **Predators include eagles,** pythons and cheetahs.

→ **The gestation period is about four weeks** and two young leverets are born.

→ **The usual lifespan** for scrub hares is about five years.

→ **The hare is often the trickster in African folktales.** Because it is small, it is able to take advantage of its size, giving the impression that it does not pose a threat to the larger and more powerful animals. Because the hare moves swiftly and is a good jumper, it is not easily caught. Known to be callous and selfish, the hare often tricks and outwits other animals in response to an act of deception by an unsuccessful trickster or it is just motivated to deceive.

Why Hen was not Eaten by Crocodile

(FJORT, CONGO)

Crocodile lived near a river that was full when the rains came, but very shallow during the dry season, exposing sandbanks all along its course.

All year round, a particular hen was in the habit of scavenging for worms at the water's edge. Sensing meat, Crocodile edged towards Hen and was about to snatch her when she cried out, 'Don't eat me, brother!'

Crocodile was perplexed and so surprised that he was being addressed in this manner that he hurried away in the opposite direction to ponder how he could be Hen's brother.

Some time later when Crocodile was resting in the shallows of the mud-brown river, looking like a floating log, he saw Hen again on the riverbank. Moving stealthily towards her, he was about to snatch her when she cried out, 'Don't eat me, brother!'

'Oh no!' shouted Crocodile angrily. 'How can I be related to you, Hen? I can't be your brother! I live in the water and you live on the land.'

Still confused, Crocodile decided to consult with Nzambi, the mother of all the animals, so that he could settle the matter and gain some understanding as to why Hen believed that they were related to each other. So he started on his long journey and on the way he met Mbambi, the large lizard.

'I'm so pleased to see you, friend,' said Crocodile. 'I'm really confused about something. When I was about to eat a succulent hen that comes to look for food at the river, she shouted out, "Don't eat me brother!"'

Lizard listened attentively.

'This happens everyday and I'm tired of it, Mbambi,' said Crocodile. 'I'm going to take my case to Nzambi so that I can get it settled.'

Lizard stared at Crocodile and said, 'Don't you dare, Crocodile. Not only will you lose the case, but you'll show your lack of knowledge and understanding.'

'How is that?' asked Crocodile, surprised.

'Crocodile, can't you see?' said Mbambi.

'See what?' said Crocodile, still confused.

'Crocodile, don't you realize that just as a duck lives in water and lays eggs, so a turtle lives in the water and lays eggs.'

'That is correct,' said Crocodile.

'I also lay eggs,' said the Lizard.

'Yes, you do,' said Crocodile.

'Can't you see that Hen also lays eggs – that is why we are all related in a way.'

At last Crocodile could see Mbambi's point and he never tried to eat that hen again.

Crocodile is Carried to the River

(WAMBO, NAMIBIA)

At a place on the western coast of Africa, some distance south of the bulge, Crocodile lay basking on a bank in the winter sun, close to a river that was the same colour as his skin.

Suddenly, the peace was disturbed by a raucous yell from Jackal, who was out to trick Hyena.

'Duiker, Kudu, Steenbuck!' said Jackal as he called out the names of animals that lived near the water.

When Hyena heard Jackal's call he became curious and trotted towards Jackal.

'I see that you are only calling the animals that have hooves! Why are you not calling those of us with pads on our feet?'

Cunning Jackal said, 'It did cross my mind, Hyena. But I've been told that you are angry with me. I believe that you are out to get me.'

Hyena kept his distance as a slight wind ruffled his tan-and-black spotted coat and the mane that moved slightly down from his shoulders. Then Jackal said, 'Hyena, I have found a skin that is very dry and I need to get it to the river to soak, only then will I be able to eat it.'

Hyena replied, 'Does that mean that you want me to take it to the river for you? I will soak it for you.'

'I would be so glad if you did that for me, Hyena. Then when you have brought it back we can eat it.'

Strong Spotted Hyena then lifted the Crocodile, straining as he hoisted it off the ground. As he was lifting the heavy weight, Crocodile sneaked a glance at Hyena.

Hyena took fright and said, 'Jackal, is that an eye or just fat?'

Black-backed Jackal reassured Hyena. 'No, it's just fat. Don't worry.'

When Hyena reached the banks of the sludge-coloured river, dragging his heavy weight, he said, 'Jackal, is this alright?'

'No, Hyena. You need to go in deeper.'

Hyena went a little deeper into the cool brown water and again asked Jackal, 'Is this deep enough?'

'Yes,' replied Jackal, his soft, browny-red coat catching the breeze that swirled above the river.

Hyena lowered Crocodile into the water and as he did so, Crocodile grabbed his front leg, threatening to drag him beneath the surface of the water. Hyena shouted at both Jackal and Crocodile, calling them names.

Then using all his strength, Hyena managed to escape the clutches of Crocodile

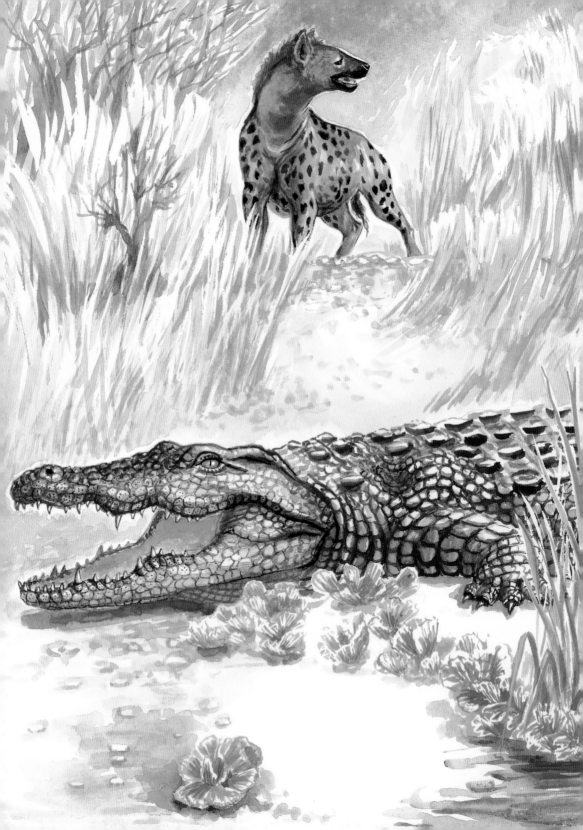

and climb out of the water. When he reached the land, he immediately went in search of Jackal who was already far away. To this day, Hyena is still searching for Jackal as he desires an explanation for his treacherous behaviour.

ZULU PROVERB

Ingweny' idl' emsingeni

The crocodile feeds at the place where the current is strong.

It is difficult to swim at the place where the current is strongest. The crocodile is partial to that place, as victims will be found there. Likewise, one should keep away from the places that one knows are evil.

Crocodile Tears

(SOUTH AFRICA)

Long, long ago, Nile Crocodile was in charge of all the water creatures and it was his duty to ensure their well-being. So, one year, when no storm clouds formed in the sky and the land was ravaged by drought, Crocodile grew worried about the animals as drinking water had become scarce.

When the river became a dry, sandy bed, Crocodile made a plan to relocate to another river that was over the next hill.

Otter was sent on a reconnaissance mission and Crocodile was delighted when he returned, saying that there was plenty of water in that place.

Crocodile then summoned Tortoise and Alligator. 'I want you to take Lion a report. It will take you a couple of days to reach your destination and you must prepare yourself well for the journey as the countryside is parched and dry and you might not find any water on the way.'

Tortoise and Alligator looked out at the hot, dry landscape and the air that shimmered above it and felt daunted by the prospect of their journey.

'We have to make peace with Lion and the animals of his kingdom,' said Crocodile. 'Otherwise we shall all die. We need Lion and his animals' assistance to move over to the other river, especially when we pass by Boer's farm.'

Tortoise and Alligator agreed with their leader. 'We water creatures can be very helpless on the land,' said Crocodile.

When he received the report, Lion was surprised by it. 'I need first to have a consultation with Jackal,' he told the messengers sent by Crocodile.

After deliberation, Lion said, 'Tomorrow night my advisors and I will be at the appointed place near the willow tree. The one that is at the furthest end of the water-hole – the place where Crocodile resides.'

Crocodile was delighted with the news that Alligator and Tortoise brought him from Lion. He arranged for Otter and a few other water creatures to be present and he organized mounds of fish and other food for the guests who would meet by the willow tree.

As the last light of the day drained away and darkness fell on the dry land, Crocodile and his water creatures warmly welcomed Lion and his entourage of Jackal, Wolf, Baboon and a few other animals. Crocodile was so overcome by the joyous occasion that every so often tears formed in his eyes and ran down his snout and onto the sandy ground.

When all the animals had feasted on the fish and the fine food, Crocodile discussed his plans with them, stating that harmony and peace amongst all the animals was needed otherwise they would destroy each other. Lion also expressed his fear that, in time, the Boer would destroy them as well. The Boer had already placed irrigation pumps at the river to water his lands and drinking water was becoming scarcer every day. Also, because the water level of the river that once flowed strongly had dropped drastically, the animals were vulnerable as they were forced to live in very shallow water.

'We are here to give you support,' said Lion, who on this occasion was sympathetic to Crocodile and his water creatures. 'I give you my word that we will escort you from the dry river bed, past Boer's farm to the river where there are sea-cow pools.'

'But what can we expect in return?' asked cunning, sly Jackal.

Crocodile thought carefully, then responded. 'Peace will be a great asset to both the water and land creatures as they will not kill each other. Also, when you land creatures arrive at the water to drink, I shall not attack you, and in turn, we will be spared Elephant's antics.'

At that point Lion and his advisor Jackal walked away from the scant shade of the willow tree for a consultation. Then Jackal said, 'Crocodile, what security will you offer to ensure that you keep your side of the agreement?'

'My word stands,' said Crocodile, as a few more tears fell into the sand.

'I think that we should trust each other,' said Baboon. 'We shall all benefit from such an agreement. What is more, the water creatures' lives are vulnerable

at this time. All we need to do, Lion, is commit everything to the written word.'

Sly Jackal did not agree with Baboon, and Wolf, who had satisfied himself with such generous helpings of fish that he was in a good mood, instructed Lion to settle the matter with the agreement.

Lion gave a speech to all assembled, announcing that they would cooperate with Crocodile and support him, as the water creatures' lives were threatened. A document was created and it was decided that the migration should start before midnight.

All the water creatures were summoned from far and wide and Lion not only organized an escort party for the animals, but he mapped the journey to the new river as well. Lion then appointed Jackal as the spy and quietly said to him, 'I am suspicious of all this. I will also be a spy until everyone reaches the sea-cow pools, but I will not be found there when you arrive.'

Elephant was delegated the role of leader because of his soft tread and good sense of smell and hearing. He was followed by Lion with one section of the animals and then Crocodile's water creatures who had protection on both sides. Wolf was at the tail end of the migration.

While travel plans were being finalized, Crocodile took the yellow snake into his confidence and said to him, 'It would be better for us if these animals were captured by the Boer. I want you to remain here and when I arrive at the sea-cow pool I will shout loudly so that you know that we have arrived at our destination.'

Snake slithered closer to Crocodile. 'Snake,' said Crocodile, 'When I scream, you must irritate the Boer's dogs and we'll see what happens next.'

The migration continued slowly in the dark and the pace was determined by many of the water creatures who were not used to travelling long distances on land. They ventured safely past the Boer's farm and by the time it was dawn, they were all safely at the sea-cow pool.

The water creatures relished the full river and quickly disappeared beneath its muddy surface.

However, before Crocodile took to the water, he thanked Lion profusely for his help, crying crocodile tears of joy. Then he asked if he might scream to let off his tense, anxious feelings that had accumulated over the journey. The mountains shook as he shouted and he then gave a lengthy delivery, outlining the advantages of the new agreement.

Just as he was about to depart, Lion heard the first shot that caused Elephant and a few other animals to keel over.

'I warned you to be cautious,' said angry Jackal. 'Why did you allow Crocodile's tears to deceive you?'

Crocodile and his water creatures were safely beneath the surface of the muddy water when a fight broke out among the animals, which made them an easy target for the Boer. Most of them survived, however.

Not long after that, Crocodile was blasted by a driver who let off some dynamite. And it is said that even to this day, whenever Elephant is given the opportunity, he throws Crocodile's descendents into the forks of trees as high up as possible.

Crocodylus niloticus

→ **Nile Crocodiles are found in Senegal** and east to Ethiopia, south to the Okavango Delta (in northern Botswana) and northern KwaZulu-Natal. They are also found in northwest Madagascar and Nosy Be, off the north west coast of Madagascar. They are no longer found along the Nile and Mediterranean coast.

→ **The Nile Crocodile is found mainly in mangrove swamps,** freshwater lakes, rivers and estuaries.

→ **The dorsal skin of the Nile Crocodile** is covered with horny plates while the skin of the belly is softer.

→ **Its hind feet are webbed** and it has a long strong tail that propels the body forward in the water.

→ **It has long jaws** with very prominent teeth.

→ **The Nile Crocodile ventures towards its prey** underwater or at water level. Its diet includes large fish, zebras, buffaloes and antelopes.

→ **Nile Crocodiles run very fast on land.**

→ **They mate in the water.** The female digs a hole and lays on average about 40 eggs with strong shells. After covering them with a layer of sand, she fasts for about three months while protecting the site. When they hatch, she carries the young in her mouth to the river where she washes them.

The Buffalo and the Bees

(WEST AFRICA)

It was while grazing one night under the watchful eye of the king of the night and his tribe of stars, that the leader of a herd of very strong buffaloes decided to move to a place where there was better grazing.

They journeyed for many days and arrived at a place where life was good. Deer had made the forest their resting place, hares found plenty of food in the fields of Man and Tortoise sunned himself on the banks of the river. The only dangers in that area were snakes that lived in the bush and lions whose roars made all the animals tremble.

But when the buffaloes arrived, they brought disaster with them. The powerful dark brown beasts that were the colour of bark, trampled the crops and destroyed them. Small animals were crushed under their heavy feet without the buffaloes even noticing them. And if it were not for their hard protective shells, even Tortoise and his family would have been destroyed.

So, the animals called a meeting to discuss what could be done.

Tortoise spoke out first, 'I think that we should approach the head of the buffalo herd and complain about all the destruction caused by his family. Then we need to ask them to inflict less damage to the land.'

The animals agreed with Tortoise and decided to go in search of the cunning head of the herd, whom they found asleep.

'He will be very angry if we wake him,' said Deer. 'Buffaloes are known to be very dangerous, especially when confronted.'

'So what!' said Lion assertively in a loud voice. 'We haven't come all this way for nothing!'

But their strong voices disturbed Buffalo and he shouted out angrily, 'Why did you wake me?'

'Sorry,' said Lion, 'but we have travelled far to see you.'

'And what do you want?' asked Buffalo, grabbing a tuft of grass.

'We have come to ask you to be more considerate,' pleaded Tortoise, keeping his distance. 'You have caused great damage, although I'm sure that was never your intention.'

Buffalo scowled at Tortoise and shook his back in anticipation of the relief he would get from the ticks on the oxpecker bird, which had just arrived.

Cautiously, Tortoise continued, 'In your stampede you have crushed birds and small creatures. Even members of my family were trampled and only survived because of their tough shells.'

Boldly Tortoise continued to speak while the buffalo leader grazed the lush grass. 'You have also destroyed Man's crops and I warn you that if he starts hunting your flesh, everyone could become victims. Please keep away from the crops and allow my family and the turtles to use a section of the riverbank.'

'And, please, be careful where you tread,' pleaded Hare.

By now Buffalo was furious. 'We are doing what we have always done. This is how we live and as rulers of the bush we are entitled to do as we please. So take care of yourselves and we shall take care of ourselves; and if Man intervenes, he'll regret it.'

Anger grew in Lion and he responded to Buffalo's arrogance by crying out in a loud voice. 'You think that you are king of the bush, but it is widely known that we lions rule the bush. Let us fight to see who is the king!'

'Stop!' pleaded Tortoise, retracting his head.

But a fight broke out between Lion and Buffalo and the animals formed a circle around them. Lion, who was past his prime, hadn't fought for a long time and all the animals feared that he would lose the duel.

Buffalo fought fearlessly. Although he had been injured by Lion, the ruler of the buffaloes pinned his opponent to the ground, broke his back and caused Lion to take his last breath.

The animals were distraught and Python seethed with anger. He believed that he was stronger than Lion and that had he fought Buffalo, he would have been successful.

'The matter is settled,' said Buffalo, staggering a little. 'I am ruler of this region. Does anyone dare to disagree with that?'

'I do,' said Python, surging towards the powerful beast to fight him. But when he realized that he was losing the fight due to injuries, he withdrew.

'This shows us that we shall have to rely on brains rather than brute force,' observed Tortoise.

'Listen,' said Hare. 'I went to Man's fields this morning and overheard him say that he wanted to get rid of the buffalo herd.'

'Then we can enlist Man's help,' said Tortoise, showing pleasure. 'I need a monkey and a queen bee,' said Tortoise, who then sent Hare to find them.

On their arrival Tortoise said, 'Please, Queen Bee, could you provide us with a hive so that we can eradicate the buffalo ruler who has caused so much damage here?'

The Queen Bee was reluctant; however, it was agreed that Monkey would fetch the hive. Tortoise then asked Hare to summon the wild pigs who were digging in the distance.

'Please dig a hole for us under that large spreading tree over there,' asked Tortoise, politely.

'What is our reward?' asked shrewd Pig.

'Getting rid of the buffalo herd!'

'Alright then,' said Pig, digging an enormous hole that was well covered and concealed with branches and leaves by the monkeys.

'This is a great trap,' said Monkey, who loved to deceive other animals.

Tortoise instructed the monkeys to get the beehive and place it next to the trap. Then Tortoise asked Monkey to go and find Buffalo who was eventually found wallowing in the muddy waters of the river.

Meanwhile Monkey sat on the bank of the river, his charcoal fur lit by the last rays of the sun and cried out loud while smearing mud all over his body.

'What is wrong with you, Monkey?' asked Buffalo, puzzled. 'You look agitated.'

'I stole some honey this morning and knocked over the hive. The bees then turned on me and stung me! Ooh! I'm in such pain. My body aches.'

Buffalo listened attentively.

'There is such a wonderful supply of honey... but I am too sick to eat it... what a shame...'

'Where is it?' asked Buffalo.

'Under that large tree.'

Buffalo left Monkey rolling in the mud and went in the direction of the honey. Monkey was not the only one watching him; Tortoise and Hare followed Buffalo with their eyes as he approached the hive. Then suddenly they heard a loud yell as Buffalo fell through the leaves into the deep, dark pit.

'We've captured him at last,' said Hare.

'But there's more to do,' said Tortoise. 'Hare, you go to the village and activate the dogs.'

When they saw Hare run by, the dogs barked excitedly and chased Hare all the way back to the large hole under the tree. And when they heard their dogs yelping, the men of the village ran after them to investigate what had happened.

'It's that Buffalo who has destroyed all our crops,' said one of the men. Let's kill him and have a feast.'

And so all the animals joined in the feast that continued throughout the night and the next day and when the rest of the herd discovered that they had lost their leader, the buffaloes moved on to new grazing. Tortoise, Hare and Monkey were delighted. So was Snake, although he was still recovering from his fight with Buffalo.

Akunyathi yahlulwa yithole

ZULU PROVERB

A buffalo is not defeated by its calf.
A buffalo finds a way of keeping its calf under control. The same is true for humans.

Syncerus caffer

→ **The Cape buffalo is found from southern Sudan** and Ethiopia, south through central and east Africa to Angola, Zambia, Zimbabwe and northeast South Africa.

→ **Buffaloes belong to the hoofed Bovidae family** that includes cattle, sheep, goats and antelopes.

→ **Bovids are an old group of animals** that have inhabited the earth for millions of years.

→ **Buffaloes eat long grass,** thus allowing zebras and wildebeest to graze with them as they prefer short grass.

→ **Buffaloes are ruminants.** They chew the cud and their four-chambered stomachs, gastric juices and very strong teeth enable them to eat tough grass.

→ **Buffaloes have distinctive curved horns.** The female's horns are thinner and shorter.

→ **They form herds** of up to several thousand.

→ **They are known to be cunning** and bad tempered.

→ **Because they are large**, buffaloes have few predators except for lions.

→ **Breeding occurs all year round** in some places; it is seasonal in others. Bulls that are past their prime form bachelor groups or become solitary.

→ **The gestation period** is about 11 to 11 and a half months and one calf is born.

→ **Traditionally, buffaloes were highly regarded** by the people of Africa because of their size and strength.

Mantis gives the Buck their Colours

(SAN, SOUTHERN AFRICA)

The Mantis, a hero in San folktales, has supernatural powers, although he is also foolish at times. Dorothea Bleek comments that 'he seems to be just a sort of dream Bushman'. ('Bushmen' is the word formerly used for the San people.)

Gemsbok, who is known for his beautiful, long, slightly curved, grey horns was once given liquid honey to eat, which is white in colour. It is said that it was Mantis who gave Gemsbok this white honey and that is why the buck is white in colour.

Then Mantis gave Red Hartebeest, who has shorter curled horns, the waxy comb of some very young bees, which contained red honey. Red Hartebeest ate this red honey and this explains why Hartebeest's coat is rich, reddish-brown in hue.

Mantis then found some wasp's honey and gave it to Eland, the buck with twists in his horns. Because the wasp's honey was darker than that of the bees, Eland's coat is darker than the other bucks'.

Then Mantis gave Quagga some dark honey, which he ate ravenously and this contributed to the dark markings on Quagga's coat.

Finally, Springbok with his ridged horns, was given the red liquid from the young bees' cells, which Mantis squeezed out of the comb drop by drop so that Springbok could get it all. That is why Springbok has rich, red-brown shiny fur.

Oryx gazella

→ **The gemsbok, which is pale grey in colour** with black patches on its upper hindlegs and rump is found from southwest Zimbabwe and southwest Angola, through Botswana and Namibia to the northern Western Cape.

→ **Gemsbok are herbivorous grazers,** eating grass and fruit, mainly wild melons and cucumbers.

→ **They have the ability to survive in areas** where there is very little water.

→ **Because gemsbok live in semi-deserts** where it is hot and dry, there is a risk that their blood might overheat and cause brain damage. To prevent this, during the day as the gemsbok's body temperature increases, the blood passes through a network of blood vessels in the nose *en route* to the brain. It is here that the blood is cooled by air breathed in by the gemsbok.

→ **Gemsbok live in herds of up to 12 individuals** and they are gregarious.

→ **The gestation period is eight and a half months** and a single calf is born without horns so that the mother is not damaged during birth.

Alcelaphus buselaphus

→ **The red hartebeest is found in Botswana,** Namibia and the Western Cape and it has also been introduced into other areas of South Africa.

→ **Both sexes have horns** and look similar.

→ **All hartebeest are able to eat high-fibre,** low-protein grass and their long, narrow, muzzles assist them in grazing selectively.

→ **They are grazers** and live in herds of up to 20 animals.

→ **Red hartebeest look awkward** when they run but they are able to achieve a speed of 60 kilometres an hour.

→ **They are often found grazing** with wildebeest, zebras and other antelopes.

→ **The gestation period is eight months** and a single calf is born.

Taurotragus oryx

→ **The eland is found in east Africa,** south to KwaZulu-Natal and Angola.

→ **It is the largest** and also the slowest antelope. Its highest speed is about 40 kilometres an hour. It is able to jump high.

→ **The eland is one of the most nomadic** of the antelopes and is found in small herds.

→ **It is a herbivorous browser** and it grasps its food with its lips rather than its tongue. Although primarily a browser, it will eat grass.

→ **The eland can survive for a month** without water and it conserves its liquid by not sweating.

→ **The gestation period is nine months** and one calf is born.

→ **The eland occurs frequently** in San rock paintings in southern Africa. Not only did it provide food for them, but they revered it as a 'supreme being' and a source of beauty.

Equus quagga

→ **It is extinct and little is known about it.** It is thought that it became extinct by the 1850s as a result of hunters and the destruction of its habitat by encroaching sheep farms.

→ **The quagga's name is derived from the Khoi name,** which phonetically replicated their call: 'kwa-ha-ha'.

Antidorcas marsupialis

→ **The springbok is cinnamon brown in colour** with white on its head, underparts, backs of legs, tail and rump. It has a dark brown, side stripe, a stripe on the cheek and a black tail tip.

→ **The springbok, or springbuck,** is found in southwestern Angola, Namibia, Botswana and South Africa.

→ **It derives its name from its 'pronking'-like motion.** It can jump with stiff legs to about three metres with its head held downwards, its back bowed and its spine erect.

→ **It is a herbivorous grazer and browser.** It browses in the dry season and can survive without water provided it obtains some water in its food. Bulbs and roots are dug for this purpose.

→ **The springbok is found in flat open country** and seldom in mountainous regions.

→ **The springbok's main predators are lions,** leopards and cheetahs, while young springbok often become the victims of black-backed jackals and eagles.

→ **The gestation period is six to seven months** and a single calf is born.

Glossary

Acacia: A mimosa-like tree that occurs in dry areas. It has white or yellow flowers and it often has thorns. Its leaves, seeds and pods have a high food value.

Boer: An Afrikaans word for farmer.

Browser: An animal that eats mainly from trees and bushes, in contrast to a grazer, an animal that eats grass.

Bush: Refers to those areas in South Africa that are still in their natural state.

Burrow: A hole dug in the ground by certain animals for shelter or defence.

Camouflage: A disguise or device for deceiving an enemy or predator. Through camouflage, an animal is able to blend in with its surroundings.

Carnivore: An animal that feeds on other animals is called a carnivore. It is described as carnivorous.

Carrion: The dead body or decaying flesh of an animal.

Crevice: A crack or narrow opening, for example in a group of rocks.

Den: A hollow or cave used by large carnivores as a shelter.

Diurnal: An animal that is active by day.

Duiker:	The grey duiker (*Sylvicapra grimmia*) is one of the hardiest antelopes in Africa, surviving where other species have become extinct. They live singly or in pairs. The blue duiker (*Cephalophus monticola*) is the smallest antelope found in southern Africa.
Estuary:	The place – usually wide – where fresh water (river) and salt water (ocean) meet.
Extinction:	A species is extinct when it has died out and completely disappeared from the earth, for example the quagga and blue antelope.
Gestation:	The period of time from conception to birth. This refers to mammals only.
Grazer:	An animal that feeds mainly on grass.
Gregarious:	Animals that live in herds or groups are called gregarious.
Grindstone:	A grindstone or grinding stone is one used for sharpening or grinding tools.
Habitat:	The natural home of an animal or plant.
Herbivore:	An animal that eats plants is called a herbivore or it is referred to as herbivorous.
Litter:	A litter refers to all the young born together (that is, two or more babies born from a single birth) and is a term only used for mammals.
Mammal:	Mammals are warm-blooded creatures that suckle their young and are at least partly covered by hair. Usually their young are born alive.
Mangrove:	Mangroves are salt-resistant shrubs and trees that are found along tropical coastlines.

Migratory: Migratory animals are those that move seasonally in search of better food and water.

Nocturnal: An animal that is active at night.

Omnivore: An animal that eats both animals and plants.

Predator: An animal that hunts and kills other animals (the prey) for its food supply.

Prey: An animal that is captured or hunted by another animal (the predator) for food.

Regurgitate: To bring back into the mouth partly digested food that has been swallowed.

Sahel: An area of very dry savanna along the southern Sahara from Mauritania, east to Sudan.

Savanna: An area of open grasslands with scattered bushes and trees that occurs in tropical regions.

Scavenger: An animal that lives off decaying flesh or the remains of another animal's kill, for example a jackal.

Solitary: An animal that lives alone as opposed to one that is gregarious.

Wallow: To roll in a mud bath.

Waterhole: A communal place for the animals to obtain water.

Bibliography

Africa –Myths and Legends, Alice Werner (Studio Editions, 1995)

African Folktales, Yoti Lane (Peter Lunn Publishers, 1946)

African Folktales and Sculpture, Paul Radin (ed.) (Bollingen Foundation, Inc., New York, 1964)

African Folktales: Traditional Stories of the Black World, Roger D. Abrahams (Pantheon Books, 1983)

African Myths and Legends, Kathleen Arnott (Oxford University Press, 2000)

A Treasury of African Folklore, Harold Courlander (Crown Publishers, 1975)

Bushman Stories, E.W. Thomas (Oxford University Press, 1950)

Daughter of the Moonlight and other African Tales, Dianne Stewart (Struik Publishers, 1994)

Folklore of Southern Africa, A.C. Partridge (Purnell, 1973)

Folktales of the Wambo, edited by J.J. Viljoen *et al* (Unisa, 1984)

Folk Stories from Southern Nigeria, Elphinstone Dayrell (Longman, Green and Co, 1910, Internet Sacred Text Archive)

Mammals of Southern Africa, Mike Nicol (Struik Publishers, 1984)

Namibia, Land and Peoples Myths and Fables, Jan Knappert (E.J. Brill, 1981)

National Audubon Society Field Guide to African Wildlife, Alden, Estes, Schlitter, McBride (Alfred A. Knopf, 1995)

Notes on the Fjort, Richard Edward Dennett (David Nutt, 1898, Internet Sacred Text Archive)

Nursery Tales, Traditions and Histories of the Zulus, Rev. Canon Callaway (Baker and Taylor Co, 1910)

South African Folk Tales, James A. Honeÿ (Baker and Taylor Co, 1910)

Tales from the Basotho, Minnie Postma, (Afrikaanse Pers-Boekhandel, 1964)

The Aquarian Guide to African Mythology, Jan Knappert (The Aquarian Press, 1990)

The King's Drum and other African Stories, Harold Courlander (Harcourt, Brace Jovanovich, 1962)

The Mantis and his Friends, D.F. Bleek (ed.) (Maskew Miller Longman, 1923)

The Zulu Folktale Tradition, Noverino N. Canonici (Zulu Language and Literature, University of Natal, 1993)

Why the Lion Roars and other African Animal Stories, G.N. Lansdown (Macmillan and Co, 1948)

Zulu Proverbs, C.L.S. Nyembezi (Shuter and Shooter, 1990)